FAR TO GO

FAR TO GO

Noel Streatfeild

A Yearling Book

Published by
Dell Publishing Co., Inc.
1 Dag Hammarskjold Plaza
New York, New York 10017

This work was first published in Great Britian by William Collins Sons & Co. Ltd.

Yearling ® TM 913705, Dell Publishing Co., Inc.

ISBN: 0-440-42494-1

Printed in the United States of America

March 1986

10 9 8 7 6 5 4 3 2 1

CW

To Sophie, who liked *Thursday's Child*

Contents

1. Far to Go

Every day when she arrived at the theater Margaret would feel a sort of blown-up feeling inside because she was so happy. To other people there might not seem much about the theater to make her happy, for it was only a tent. It had started life—many years before—with a little family circus who had grandly called it "The Big Top." That circus had done well, so the owner had bought a bigger tent and had advertised for a buyer for his old one. The advertisement had been seen by Mr. Fortescue, actor-manager of the Fortescue Comedy Company, who acted in what was called a fit-up theater, that is to say, they put up a stage and curtains and acted in any building which could be rented where they could find an audience. It was the proudest moment in Mr. Fortescue's life when in 1895 he had bought the big tent and had had "Fortescue Comedy Company" painted on it.

Margaret could not go to the theater until the afternoons, for she had to attend the local school. She did not mind, for she loved school, not just for the lessons but because she was special there. Not that she needed to be told she was special, for she had always known that she was so. Who else had been found in a basket when they were a baby, with three of everything, all of the very best quality? Who else had a card sent with her which said, "This is Margaret whom I entrust to your care"? Who else had received fifty-two golden sovereigns each year for her keep? Margaret knew it was not because of this romantic start to her life that the children admired her; it was because they had seen her act Little Lord Fauntleroy, and they thought she was wonderful.

Oddly enough, that part of Margaret who was proud of herself did not care if she was admired as an actress or not. Acting was a different thing altogether. It was something that came to you when you stepped on the stage that made you forget everything except the part you were acting, that made you believe what you were saying and turned all the other actors into the people they were meant to be, so she never, when on the stage, saw them as the tawdry, seedy bad actors, atrociously dressed, that they really were.

At the back of the theater in a small tent, Mrs. Sarah Beamish spent her days. She was a wonderfully good needlewoman and so was in charge of the wardrobe, though she played character parts or walked on when needed. Sarah had taken Margaret under her wing when she had joined the company four months before and, in innumerable ways, had not only seen after her but, when necessary, fought for her welfare. It was Sarah Beamish who saw that she attended school. Her fat little figure had waddled into Ida Fortescue's—the leading lady and manageress—dressing tent a few nights after *Little Lord Fauntleroy* had become part of the repertory. Ida was taking off her makeup and did not want to be interrupted.

"Well?"

"Young Margaret should go to school starting Monday," said Sarah.

The question of sending Margaret to school had been discussed by the Fortescues, and they had decided against it. In the company there was an actress so short, she was almost a dwarf, who had played children when they were needed. She had no talent, so the Fortescues had decided, as soon as the summer was over, to dismiss her and give the parts to Margaret, which would mean that she would be needed for morning rehearsals. Now what was Sarah Beamish sticking her nose in for? However, Sarah was too valuable in the wardrobe to be treated rudely. Ida spoke as though her tongue had been covered with cream.

"Do you not think that a long role every night is enough for her? She is only just eleven."

Sarah was not fooled by a creamy voice.

"No, I do not. I think she should have proper schooling like any ordinary child. Besides, it's the law. Very strict they say they are now about children's schooling."

This was a brave statement from Sarah, who had not the faintest idea about school and the law. When she had grown up, some children were still working in the cotton mills. She had herself for a year when her father had been out of work through an injury, but times were changing fast, and now, with the coming of a new century, life was much easier for children. Even girls going into service in private houses seldom went until they were twelve.

As a result of what Sarah had said, Margaret had been sent to the village school. Ida Fortescue had settled the argument.

"What does it matter, Mr. Fortescue?" she had said to

11

her husband. "It's just coming to the autumn. If we can get an audience in our tent for *Fauntleroy* until October, we've done grand. Come mid-October we have to move under a roof, anyway, and what school there may be there we can wait and see."

As she said this she winked to show her husband that there would be no schooling for Margaret if she was needed for theater work.

Now it was late September, the last week when they could use a tent. It was pleasant weather with just a nip in the air to remind everyone that summer was coming to an end and, in Margaret's case, to put a skip into her walk and make her hum a tuneless song to the words "I do like being me."

Sarah heard her coming.

"Is that you, Margaret?" she called.

Margaret ran the last few steps and flung her arms around Sarah's neck.

"Of course it's me, who else would it be? You know everybody is having a nap. Were you wanting me? What can I do?"

Sarah had a small kettle under which the water was heated by a spirit lamp. Now she lit it.

"We'll have a cup of tea first and then I've something I want to talk to you about."

Margaret groaned.

"How mean! Why not talk first and then tea? You know how I hate waiting to hear things. Hannah, the one who brought me up—"

Sarah stopped her.

"Now don't start on about how the rector found you and Hannah brought you up. I know that." Her voice softened. "Though very nicely that Hannah managed, I will say, but now we've other things to talk of. Open my cotton box and you will find a bag of sweet biscuits."

It seemed to Margaret an intolerable time before the kettle boiled, but really it was only a matter of minutes before she and Sarah were drinking tea and eating the fancy biscuits. Margaret had grown to know Mrs. Beamish, as she respectfully called her, too well in the past four months to hope to hurry her, but she watched her, quivering like an eager puppy, and at last she had her reward. Sarah felt in her apron pocket and brought out a piece cut from a newspaper.

"I haven't talked about your future, Margaret, because there has not been any cause."

"There isn't now," said Margaret.

Sarah went on as if she had not been interrupted.

"That's as may be, but some thinks different."

"But I know we're leaving this tent next week and that it is being stored in a barn until next spring. Mr. Fortescue has booked a hall where we move to and we play repertory until Christmas, when we put on pantomime, and I shall be a little white cat and—"

Sarah stopped her with an upraised hand.

"I am aware of what is planned, but maybe others have plans too." Her tone changed. "Listen, dear, I'm not the only one who has been watching you. I know you are not one to let compliments go to your head, but since you took on playing Little Lord Fauntleroy you've shown yourself an actress. Mind you, talent in a child does not mean talent when you've grown up, but I am not the only one in the company who has real hope for you." Sarah paused and unfolded the piece of paper. "So when I saw this I said to myself: 'Sarah Beamish, it's meant.' "

Margaret held out her hand.

"What is it, Mrs. Beamish? Show me."

Sarah passed her a cutting from a theatrical paper called *The Era*. Margaret unfolded it and read: "Wanted: A clever girl to appear eleven. Appointment, write to Thomas Smith, The Dolphin Theater."

"Where is The Dolphin Theater?"

Sarah smiled at such ignorance.

"In London, of course. It belongs to Sir John Teaser. He is what they call a theatrical manager, which means he owns his own company and acts as well. Very important man Sir John is. Why, when he went to Buckingham Palace for Queen Victoria to make him a knight, hundreds turned out to see him in his carriage drive through the palace gates."

Margaret reread the cutting from the paper.

"I shouldn't think he would see me. I mean, London must be full of child actresses."

Sarah nodded.

"I thought that. A big man like Sir John Teaser would only have to raise a little finger and he'd have his theater crammed full of clever little girls, all frills and curls with their mothers pushing them on. So, I say to myself, he's looking for something different, and maybe the answer is Margaret. She is eleven, not just appearing to be, and she is clever, sometimes too clever by half."

Margaret felt a glow of excitement; it was a very small glow, more like a spark, which could start a fire.

"Just in case I was the girl he wants, how do I get to London? Because I haven't any money, at least almost

14

none, because Mr. Fortescue engaged me as a student all found, which doesn't mean more than my bed and food and a few clothes like the frocks you've made me and. . ."

"How you do run on," said Sarah. "You might give me credit for a little sense. Of course I know you haven't any money, but I have my savings, not much in this company, of course, but I used to earn more—"

Margaret stopped her, eyes flashing as though a light were shining behind them. She threw her chin into the air.

"Thank you very much, but I don't want charity. You forget I was found in a basket with three of everything all of the very best quality and—"

Sarah stopped her.

"I know. Now calm down, do. I wasn't offering to give you the money, only lend it. You can pay me back when you're earning. Now listen. I've got a sister called Louisa, but we just call her Lou. She works in a theater wardrobe department. Well, her theater puts on pantomime at Christmas, tremendous big shows they are with all of two hundred *artistes*. So, well, before Christmas the wardrobe mistress hires dozens of extra staff to work on the *panto* dresses. Many's the time Lou has written to me begging me to work with her over Christmas so we could see each other like. Each year I mean to go, but somehow I never have. But this year I'm going. I sent Lou a letter saying to expect us Monday, and I wrote to this Thomas Smith asking for an appointment. I gave Lou's address."

2. The Postcard

Sarah and Margaret traveled to London after dark so that no member of the company would see them go. The station was quite near the hall where the Fortescue company was playing *Maria Martin*, or *The Murder in the Red Barn*. It was always popular and, such scenery as there was, easy to set on the stage, so they usually opened a season with it. There was no part in the play for Margaret so no one would miss her, but Sarah's and Margaret's, hearts beat very fast as they crept out of their lodgings and down the village street. When they reached the station, they hid behind the shed where left luggage was stored, but even so, and though it was not likely that any member of the company would come to the station at that time of night, they clung to each other, jumping at every sound.

When at last they were safely in an empty carriage and the train was chugging out of the station, Sarah let out a breath so held in that as it came out, her jet necklace rattled.

"It's not that I think what we're doing is wrong," she whispered. "I mean, Mr. Fortescue couldn't have stopped us going if we wanted to."

Margaret agreed.

"Of course it's not you, it's me. I don't suppose I can leave just when I want to. I'm only a student and I did sign a paper."

"Well, we needn't trouble about that now," said Sarah hopefully. "I can't see Mr. Fortescue going to the police, he never would."

"Well, he can't if he wants to, he doesn't know where I've gone. Funny, I always seem to be running away. Did I tell you about escaping on the canal?"

"You did, I don't know how many times, and I'm not going to hear it now. We're going to settle down and have a sleep, for we have walking to do when we get to London."

London, even in the evening, seemed very crowded to Margaret. The traffic was almost all horse-drawn, and to Margaret, crouching against Sarah for safety, it seemed as if at any moment everything would spill onto the pavement, especially the great carts filled to overflowing with garden produce making their way to Covent Garden. As for the people! It seemed as if all Londoners went out walking at night. Margaret was to learn to love London in all its moods, but that night she was tired, and the unexpected rush and roar were too much for her. Not that she complained, she would never do that, but she did tremble, and Sarah, in spite of her thick, full skirt and innumerable petticoats, felt this and sympathized and took, for her, a world-shaking decision.

"We will take a cab to Lou's," she said.

The cab, when at last they got one, smelled of hay, for a sackful was under the seat for the horse's dinner, but after the noise in the street, to Margaret it was pure paradise. However, she did not overlook her arrangement with Sarah.

"Don't forget to add what this costs to what I owe you, Mrs. Beamish."

Sarah smiled.

"When you have work, we'll fix everything," she said comfortably. "There's one thing I've been thinking of, though. You can call me Sarah from now on. You see, all Lou's friends just call her Lou and they will call me Sarah. You see, Mrs. is what I call myself like. Many do in the profession when they are not so young as they were."

"Is it far to Lou's house, Sarah?" Margaret asked, emphasizing the name.

"No, dear, it's near Covent Garden. That's where the fruit and that is going. It's a big market. But you told me you had been to London before, so you must remember Covent Garden."

In the darkness Margaret blushed. She knew that sometimes she exaggerated to make a better story.

"I have, but I didn't stay the night. You see, Hannah, the one who brought me up after the vicar found me on the church steps—"

"With three of everything of the very best quality," Sarah quoted.

"That's right," Margaret agreed. "Well, she had to bring me to London to the third-class waiting room at Paddington Station. There a terrible woman from the orphanage met us."

"So that's all of London you've ever seen?"

"That's right," said Margaret.

Sarah took one of Margaret's hands in hers.

"Now don't worry, love, we'll soon be at Lou's, and if I

18

know her, she'll have taken the time off to welcome us and there'll be tripe and onions for supper, and until you've tasted Lou's tripe and onions, you haven't lived."

Afterward Margaret could not remember much about the arrival at Lou's. She remembered climbing innumerable stairs at the top of which stood Lou. She was very like Sarah but twice as fat. She remembered the smell of tripe and onions, which filled Lou's room at the top of the stairs, and she remembered Lou and Sarah hugging each other while Lou said: "A card's come, they're seeing her tomorrow," and shoved a card into Margaret's hands. On it Margaret read:

DOLPHIN THEATER
Mr. Thomas Smith
will see
Miss Margaret Thursday
on Tuesday next at 11:30

3. The Red Dress

Sir John and Lady Teaser and their daughter lived in spacious apartments over The Dolphin Theater. It was, Sir John found, infinitely less tiring to live where he worked than to have to drive to and fro to somewhere more fashionable, which was what Lady Teaser would have liked.

That Tuesday morning Sir John was enjoying a late breakfast when Lady Teaser swept into the room. She gave him a kiss.

Lady Teaser—her name was Ada—was an imposing-looking woman of a statuesque type. She had been an actress and had made a name for herself in a small way. But when she married Sir John Teaser, she had given up her career, for she was sure, if they both put their minds to it, that John would rise to be head of his profession. Because she had stopped acting, that did not mean that she had lost all ambition; she was very, very conscious that if she had gone on, she, too, might have reached the heights. Anyone who knew her and forgot this was making a very great mistake.

Now, as she had come in and because the day was beautiful, and Ada, judging by the kiss, in a good temper, Sir John turned the conversation to his new play.

"I have left the sorting out of possible little girls to Tommy—he won't let any of promise pass by him—but it is proving difficult to find exactly the child I want. He has had no luck so far. I gather they are all curls and dimples."

There was a pause, which Sir John prayed Ada would fill, but when she spoke, it was not to say what he wished to hear.

"If you are still hoping I will allow Katie to play the part, you are wasting your time. Our little girl is being brought up to be a fashionable young lady. When she is old enough, she will be presented at Court, and later she will marry a suitable husband, preferably a member of the peerage—"

Sir John laid a hand on Ada's shoulder.

"I know, dear, that is what you hope, but think back to the old days when you were an ambitious child. Imagine what you would have felt if you had been given the chance to play the leading part in a beautiful play."

Ada shook his hand off her shoulder.

"When I was a child, the question did not arise, and if it had, my father would not even have considered it."

Sir John tactfully did not point out that Ada's father, a poor man, would probably have jumped at the offer.

"I shall not override your wishes, Ada, you know that, but I do beseech you to think of Katie. She is an exceptionally gifted child, and though she has heard nothing from either of us about the part of Anastasia, there must be talk, you know what servants are."

Ada nodded.

"If necessary, I will tell Katie the whole truth. She will be angry with me for she believes herself to be an actress, but I do not want Katie to lead the life we led. You may have forgotten, but I have not, those dreadful theatrical lodgings in which we stayed when we were first married. The mice and the rats"—she shuddered—"the vermin in the beds where we lodged. By the time Katie was born, things had improved a little, and although, when small, she traveled with us, I suspect she has forgotten the discomforts and the smells. I have only one daughter. Is it not natural I should wish to keep her away from those sordid things that you and I remember?"

Sir John knew he was beaten. He took his watch out of his pocket.

"I'm going down to see what news Tommy has. I believe he's seeing another child this morning."

Lou had only one room. She shared the kitchen and lavatory with the fourteen other tenants. Fortunately her bed was big, so Sarah squeezed in with her. Margaret slept on a borrowed mattress on the floor.

Because the sisters were both members of the profession, as they grandly described being actresses, the next morning belonged to Margaret. Seeing a manager about a part was important, and everyting else had to be put on one side for it.

First there was a discussion about Margaret's hair. For Fauntleroy it had been dyed with peroxide, but now the dye was growing out, and Margaret's original chestnut hair was showing at the roots. Lou ran her fingers through Margaret's curls.

"Lovely hair it is."

"If I slip out quick," said Sarah, "I could get more peroxide. Wouldn't take long to do."

Lou thought about that.

"Very high-class The Dolphin is. I wouldn't think that Sir John would fancy dyed hair, not on a child."

Sarah gave in.

"After all, this Mr. Smith who is seeing her will be used to hair dyes and that, seeing as it's a theater, so he'll know it could be fixed whatever color was wanted."

Next came the problem of what Margaret was to wear. The choice was small. She owned one blue pleated skirt worn with a darker blue knitted jersey. Both were the worse for wear. She had two cotton frocks made for her by Sarah. They were of the cheapest cotton but more or less in the fashion, for they came well below the knees and both had a little frill around the bottom, but it was too late in the year for cotton frocks. There were also two pinafores beautifully made by Sarah from some odds and ends of muslin and lace left over from stage dresses.

"The cotton frocks are out, said Sarah, "for she hasn't got a coat."

Lou was not a person who gave in easily. After all, was she not second to the wardrobe mistress at the London Hippodrome, where could be seen the most lavish production of *Cinderella* ever staged? Now, easing herself into the only chair big enough for her, she gave herself to deep thought.

"She's a rare one for seein' the way out of blind alleys is Lou," Sarah whispered, "which, of course, she often has to do in her position."

Suddenly Lou, who had for a few minutes appeared to be asleep, jerked upright.

"I have it. There's me crimson. I don't know when I last wore it."

She forced herself out of the chair, went to her cupboard, and, after some fumbling, produced an armload of dress. It was made of material called bombazine and was the same red as a mailbox. She had worn it in the days of bustles, so there was a quantity of material in it.

"There!" she said. "Isn't that striking?" It was indeed striking, perhaps too striking, for she added, "She could wear one of her pinnies over it. That would tone it down."

"Can we make it in time?" Sarah asked doubtfully.

Lou looked despisingly at her sister.

"Time! I could make four in time if I had to. Now clear the table. . . ."

They pulled the table out from the wall and pushed aside the remains of breakfast. Then Lou lifted the dress onto the table.

"I'll cut it out, then you tack it together, Sarah, then I can run it around to the theater to finish it on one of their sewing machines. You have an iron ready to press it, and it will all be Sir Garnet."

And, as far as Sarah was concerned, it was all Sir Garnet when at 11:25 A.M. she and Margaret arrived at the stage door of The Dolphin Theater. Margaret was less happy. She was not herself in the scarlet frock, which was somehow stuffy and clung to her in the wrong places.

"Cheer up, dear," said Sarah, "you look ever so nice. I'm sure they'll take you." Then she opened the stage door and said to the doorkeeper, "Miss Thursday with an appointment to see Mr. Smith."

24

4. The Interview

Sir John was with his manager, Tommy Smith, when the message was received that Margaret had arrived.

"Then I will get out of the way," said Sir John.

"Stay and see the child," Tommy pleaded. "Then you will understand what an impossible task you've given me. I've seen dozens but they are all curls and smiles. No character in any of them."

"I could not be fair to any child," Sir John objected, "for you know my heart is set on Katie."

"Is Her Ladyship adamant?" Tommy asked.

"Absolutely. I've pleaded with her until I am exhausted. Katie is not to go on the stage."

Tommy smiled.

"I would lay a bet that when she is grown-up, Miss Katie will have her own views about that."

Outside the door there was whispering.

"No, thank you, Sarah. I will see Mr. Smith myself."

"I do think I should come in, dear, it's not seemly you going on your own."

"All the same, I shall go alone."

Then there was a knock on the door.

When she was wearing her skirt and jersey, Margaret's

dyed hair was not too noticeable, but when it was seen against a bright scarlet frock, the effect was startling. And when, to finish off the outfit, there were thin legs in black woolen stockings and black boots, poor Margaret was a figure of fun.

Sir John gave Tommy a look and buried his face in his handkerchief. Tommy hid his behind a letter.

Margaret had not liked the idea of the red dress from the beginning. Nor had she wanted her hair dyed for Fauntleroy, though she had liked the effect when it was done, so she did not need even well-disguised sniggers to tell her how she appeared to the two men. Carefully she closed the door so Sarah would not hear, then, her eyes blazing and her chin in the air, she stormed toward Tommy's desk.

"All right—laugh. I may look funny to you. I had nothing they thought suitable for me to wear to come and see you. So Lou—she's Sarah's sister—cut up her own dress to make me this frock, and my hair is dyed because I was acting Lord Fauntleroy, but when the dye is out, it's brown like a chestnut. Oh, yes, and I suppose you think the boots are funny with this red dress, but they're all I have, and if you want to know, I hate boots. But I am not a charity child, though I was once in an orphanage. I was found by the rector in a basket with three of everything all of the very best quality and money was sent every year for my keep and . . . and . . ."

There, to her shame, Margaret had to stop for she was overtaken by grief. She had felt like a person with the Fortescue Company, accepted by them all as an actress, and now these sniggering men! Swallow as she would, she could not stop the tears that poured down her cheeks.

Sir John was not a loving father for nothing. He came to Margaret and lifted her face in his hands.

"You were right to be angry. We were very rude to smile. But being angry may have helped you. Anastasia, in the play I am casting, has to be angry, and when she is angry, she should look very much like you. Now let us start all over again."

An hour later a triumphant Margaret and Sarah left The Dolphin Theater, Margaret clutching the script of *The Little Queen.* She had not been promised the part, but there was a good chance for her, and at the worst she was to have the understudy.

"You will get two pounds a week to understudy," Tommy explained, "and four pounds if you play the part."

Sarah had been brought in to hear the arrangements, and she plucked up her courage to ask a question.

"If she is engaged, could she have a small advance for clothes?"

Margaret was furious.

"I don't need charity, thank you. I've got my skirt and jersey and—"

"But no coat," Sarah pleaded, "and the winter coming on."

Sir John, who had stayed for this discussion, broke in. "I'm sure I can help there. I have a little girl just your age. I will speak to Lady Teaser. I'm sure she has cupboards full of frocks and fal-lals she will never use." He saw Margaret's eyes beginning to flash. "Don't be angry with me, it's a very sensible suggestion, for I am sure Mrs. Beamish here will be able to alter them to fit you. Then you can keep that red dress for parties."

"Study the part at the pages I've marked," said Tommy.

"Then come back at three o'clock tomorrow and perhaps we will have some clothes ready for you."

Margaret had the last word.

"I could manage. My jersey and skirt are quite good, and I expect I could buy a secondhand coat."

When Margaret and Sarah had gone, Tommy and Sir John solemnly shook hands.

Then Sir John said, "If she can lose her temper when she's acting as she does in life, that little girl is the find of the new century."

Katie was in her own way a beauty. She wore her hair cut very short, almost like a boy's. It was rather fine hair, and her mother believed that if she wore it as short as a child, it would be thick and glossy when she grew up. She was a quiet, studious child with her head always buried in a book. Her mother said she was a great reader, but Katie and her governess, Miss Grey, knew the books she read were mostly play scripts passed on to the schoolroom secretly by the theater manager, whom she called Uncle Tommy. She also read and reread Shakespeare's plays and knew most of the women's parts by heart.

Miss Grey was the daughter of a country parson. Her mother was dead, and she came in the middle of a family of nine, and though the rectory where she was brought up was rent-free, the rector's income was only one hundred pounds a year, so there were never even half pennies to spare. But the rectory children had good brains and were determined to be educated. All the boys got scholarships to schools that offered special places to the sons of clergy, and the girls learned all the village school could teach them and then taught themselves from books.

28

In addition, they learned a lot that no books could have taught them. How to stretch the hundred pounds so that they had enough to eat and were all covered, if not exactly dressed. As an aid to this, the girls ran around barefoot even in the worst weather, so that there were boots for the boys to take to school. Some sort of footwear they had every Sunday and for school, but these were curious home-made efforts. Those boys who were still at day school always walked to their school with their boots hung around their necks, only putting them on when the school was in sight.

The girls were good, too, with food. Everything that was edible and that grew wild was gathered in. They caught fish in a stream and snared rabbits. Miss Grey could keep Katie happy for hours describing her childhood.

"It was hard, I suppose," she would say, "but we were happy and people were good to us. They loved my papa and would pass it on to us in little gifts of vegetables or perhaps eggs, and the squire gave us the run of his library for books. And we have all done well. I have three brothers who are doctors and two are in the Indian Civil Service, and all my sisters are well and happily married."

"I'm glad you're not married," Katie would say. "I'm so glad you have come to look after me."

"Coming here was just what I wanted," Miss Grey would say. "Although as a child I never went to a theater, I always longed to. I read whatever I could find about the theater, but there is not much written. Then I saw your father's advertisement in *The Times* newspaper. It gave his name and I went for an interview. I never thought he would take me for, now that everybody is to be educated, teachers are expected to be trained and play the piano, and certainly have fluent French and perhaps dancing . . ."

Katie laughed at the thought of Miss Grey in her thick shoes worn sizes too big because she was used to running around barefoot, trying to teach dancing.

"But I have outside teachers for all those, it's you as a person I need. Papa was quite right, you are just perfect for me."

That evening Sir. John asked Ada about Katie's old clothes.

"I am hoping the child will do. She speaks nicely, but it seems she was brought up by two ladies, and there is some romantic story about being found in a basket: Tommy says it will do for the newspapers if the child proves suitable. But something must be done about her clothes. She could not even attend rehearsals in what she has. Has Katie any old clothes and could someone fit out the child?"

Katie was charmingly dressed in soft fabrics in pastel shades, and to her mother, dressing her was rather like dressing a doll, but the real fun was when there were new clothes to be made. Any day now she was planning to take Katie to the dressmaker to order her a winter ward-robe. Invariably, when a new season came around, what she always described as "that comical Miss Grey" would say: "Oh, but there is a cupboard full of clothes scarcely worn." How convenient that this child has turned up now! She would give orders. Miss Grey was to fit the girl out.

"You see to it, Miss Grey," she said. "Any of Katie's old clothes should do, though not, of course, party frocks."

Miss Grey went back to the schoolroom, where she had

left Katie writing an essay. She had closed the door, but even so, she lowered her voice just in case Lady Teaser should be passing.

"This afternoon the child they think will act in the new play is coming to try on some of your old clothes. Your mother did not mention you, but knowing how you enjoy meeting theater folk, I thought you might help me choose frocks for her."

Katie seemed in one second to change from a rather bored child into a radiant one. The day, which, like most days, had stretched drearily ahead for her, suddenly became special.

"Oh!" she said. "Thank you, Miss Grey. Wouldn't it be perfect if we could become friends?"

5. About the Play

The moment they reached Lou's room, Sarah wanted to go out again to Lou's theater to tell her the great news, but Margaret would not go with her.

"I've got to read this whole play before tomorrow. Sir John Teaser said so."

Sarah did not want to leave Margaret alone, but after giving her strict instructions about locking the door and not opening it to anyone, she at last left, and Margaret stretched out on the floor to read the play. On the first page was written *The Little Queen*—a play in four acts." The play opened with the child Anastasia and her father and mother returning from her grand-father's funeral. Reading what Anastasia said, Margaret decided she liked her, for she had her own views about everything and did not like being dictated to. Then Anastasia asked who were all the hundreds of people who had attended her grandfather's funeral, and her father explained.

Her grandfather was born crown prince of a small country in Eastern Europe called Parthenia. But he never came to the throne, for there was a revolution during which the then king was killed, and he escaped to England, which was his mother's country. There his son, Anastasia's father, was born and brought up.

Then Aastasia's mother took up the story. "It's been very lucky for you," she told Anastasia, "that Parthenia had that revolution, for if not, Papa would be king and I would be queen and you would be a princess and expected to behave like one, no tomboy ways such as you have at home and at school. You could never run around free, as you do now."

Then her father broke in. "You would be waited on hand and foot and everyone would curtsy or bow when they spoke to you."

To this Anastasia said, "What nonsense! I would not allow it." Margaret thought that a splendid answer, for she would not allow it, either.

Margaret went back to the play.

Then Anastasia's father explained about the hundreds of people who had come to the funeral. They were Parthenians living in exile in England but all longing to get back to Parthenia. "Which I suppose they never will," Anastasia said. Her father hesitated before he answered that. "Never is a long time. They say things are changing in Parthenia, so perhaps someday they can go home." Anastasia's mother got to her feet when he said that and gasped. "Pray God it never happens." Then she fainted and that was the end of Act I.

Margaret found Act II much less interesting, for Anastasia did not come into it and it was full of long speeches about liberty and brotherhood. But she liked the end of the act. A man who worked on Anastasia's father's estate came running in holding a pigeon. The man said the pigeon was very exhausted, it had just flown in and had a message attached to its leg. Her father took the message off the pigeon and read it. Then he said, "Ladies and gentlemen, Parthenia is free." The directions said, there was a slight pause for the news to sink in, then one of the men called out "God save the King," and as the curtain fell, everyone knelt or curtsied.

The third act opened in a hotel on the frontier of Parthenia. There were a lot of people beautifully dressed waiting to receive their new king and queen and the princess, and there were several long speeches about freedom, which Margaret skipped again. Then the stage directions said there were sounds of carriages and postilions outside the hotel, doors were thrown open, the bowing staff backed into the hotel lobby, followed by the king, the queen, and Anastasia. This dignified procession is spoiled by one of the backing staff falling over his sword and landing flat on his face. Everyone is shocked, and he is hurriedly picked up, but to Anastasia it is funny, and she lets out a peal of laughter. In an icy voice her father says to one of the ladies, "Countess, will you take the princess to her room."

Anastasia is furious. "Such nonsense!" she said. "He isn't hurt. Why shouldn't I laugh? And why should I go to my room? You said I had to come to your coronation and I've come, but I won't be pushed away into my bedroom. And though I'm sure the countess is a very nice lady, it's no good calling her my governess. All she can teach me is embroidery, she said so herself, and I hate sewing."

Margaret was so carried away by this speech that she read it through twice and did not hear Sarah tapping on the door while she called out, "Margaret, it's me."

Sarah had brought the supper in with her. It was jellied eels, something Margaret had never eaten before but which she thought delicious. Margaret told her about the play, reading to her the speech in which she lost her temper.

"No wonder you said Sir John Teaser said it might be a good thing for you losing your temper," said Sarah. "I can see now Lou and me was right. He doesn't want a pretty little thing all curls and that. He wants a child with spirit. Oh, I do hope you get the part, dear."

After supper Sarah made Margaret go to bed.

"I'll lay out Lou's supper for when she comes in, but you get a good night so you're fresh for the morning. Did you tell me you had a petticoat and drawers with lace on them? Better let me run an iron over them, for you'll need them for trying on little Miss Teaser's things."

Margaret did not at once get out her luggage basket, for she was thinking. Then she said, "That Hannah that brought me up, when she heard I was being sent to an orphanage, made for underneath three of everything."

"Because that's what you came with when you were found in a basket?"

"That's right, but as well she made one petticoat and one pair of drawers with lace on for Sundays. I never wore my own clothes in that awful orphanage. But each Sunday while I was with the Fortescues I did. But tomorrow isn't a Sunday. Do you think Hannah would mind?"

Sarah put herself in Hannah's place.

"I think if we could ask her, she would say there must be an exception to every rule."

Margaret was charmed.

"That's exactly what Hannah would think. She was always saying things like 'A stitch in time saves nine.' "

"If she made the lace underwear for Sundays," Sarah suggested, "why not wear your plain ones next Sunday to pay back, like?"

Margaret thought that splendid.

"You do have good ideas, Sarah. But I'll tell you one you haven't had. I don't mind going to bed now if that's what you want, but I'm not going to sleep until I know the end of the play. I simply couldn't."

Margaret went to bed on her mattress and rolled over so the script of the play was on her pillow. Then she read her favorite speech once more. *Oh, I do hope I am Anastasia*, she thought. *I can hear me saying that.*

In the play there was, of course, a shocked pause after Anastasia's outburst, then her father said to all the ladies and gentlemen, "Leave us, please. I wish to speak alone with my daughter."

The next scene Margaret thought rather mushy. She did not like the way Anastasia gave in to her father. If it had been her, she would have had a lot more to say. Anastasia's father talked about her duty. He told her she was called to a high position, so must behave always with that in mind. The situation in Parthenia was difficult. There were still many people, particularly the peasants, who did not want their royal family back, so it was up to all of them to behave beautifully at all times so that the country could learn to be proud of them. Then he told her that all the ladies and gentlemen who had greeted them were their loyal friends, and it would have shocked them that she could behave so badly, so he was now calling them back so that she could apologize.

There was a lot of description then, which Margaret skipped, but all the ladies and gentlemen came back, and Anastasia stood at the bottom of the staircase, facing them, and said she was sorry but she had been brought up in England where everybody said what they thought. When that was over, the ladies and gentlemen drew back, and the king and queen, followed by Anastasia, started to climb the stairs. Then there was a pistol shot and the king fell. The queen flung herself on him and said he was dead. Anastasia clung to the bannister frozen (so the script said) with terror, and then a man called out, "Long live the queen," and this was taken up by all. Anastasia suddenly realized that it was she they were calling queen. With tears pouring down her face she managed to bow to the kneeling ladies and gentlemen, then the curtain fell. But that was as far as Margaret got, for her head had rolled onto the script and she was fast asleep.

Sarah smiled as she gently slid the script away.

Pretty dear, she thought. *I do hope she gets to play the part.*

6. Katie

The next morning, while Sarah was ironing her lace-trimmed underclothes, Margaret finished reading the play. The last act was, she discovered, laid in a great cathedral, where Anastasia was being crowned. There were descriptions that made it clear it was a very colorful spectacle. There were fanfares of trumpets when Anastasia, followed by her lady attendants, entered, the ladies carrying a gold canopy over her head.

"Sarah," Margaret called out, "did you ever see a coronation?"

Sarah laughed.

"No, dear, I wasn't born when the queen was crowned, but my mother talked about it, for there were great goings-on to celebrate, like. Mother had a mug with the queen's picture painted on. Why are you asking?"

"It's Anastasia in this play, it's her coronation at the end."

"My word!" said Sarah. "That will be good news for theater people. Take a hundred or more extras or so to put that on, I shouldn't wonder."

Margaret went back to the play. Anastasia's procession had now reached a high priest, and the choir was singing.

There was then the coronation service, which finished with Anastasia being crowned. Then Anastasia faced her people to say, "I, your lawful queen, do solemnly swear that with God's help I will do my duty." Then bells pealed, the choir sang, trumpets sounded, and the curtain fell. Margaret was so carried away by all this that she believed she was Anastasia and was quite shocked when Sarah, handing her the ironed underclothes, didn't curtsy.

When Sarah and Margaret arrived at The Dolphin that afternoon, the doorkeeper greeted them like friends,

"You're to go straight to the stage. That's two floors down. You can't miss it, it's wrote up all the way."

Mr. Smith was on the stage waiting for them. Sir John Teaser was in the dress circle, but he called out, "Good afternoon, Margaret. Mr. Smith will show you what you are to read to me."

The stage seemed enormous to Margaret, for it looked even bigger than it was with only rehearsal gaslights turned on.

They started with a bit of the first act, where Anastasia came back from the funeral. Mr. Smith read the part of Anastasia's father and mother. Then, to Margaret's joy, she was told to read the scene in the third act where Anastasia lost her temper.

"Can I start from where the man falls over?" Margaret asked.

"Do," Mr. Smith agreed, "but don't expect me to fall over on this dusty stage."

To Margaret that scene was clear in her mind. Anastasia would be bored by all the fuss, probably wishing she was back at school, and then something funny happened.

Mr. Smith, bowing, came in backward through an imaginary door. Then he tripped and pointed down so Margaret could see that he was meant to be on the floor. Margaret picked up her cue. She had a very infectious laugh and now, in her mind, as she saw the courtier on the floor, she let it peal out. She was stopped by Mr. Smith, as the king, saying, "Countess, will you take the princess to her room." How mean, thought Margaret, why shouldn't she laugh? So she faced Mr. Smith with her chin high and her eyes blazing. She did not need her script for that scene, so she threw it on the stage and with fury turned on Mr. Smith.

After that speech Sir John called out something Mr. Smith did not hear, so he went to the footlights where he could hear more clearly.

"I'm coming down, Tommy," Sir John said. "I don't need to hear any more."

Sir John came onto the stage through an iron pass door. He came straight to Margaret and took her hand in his.

"Well done, dear," he said. "You will have to work very hard, but I am sure you can do it. The part is yours." Then he turned to Tommy. "Is Miss Grey here?"

"I'm here," Miss Grey's voice answered. "Come up, dear, and, of course, you too," she said to Sarah. "And we'll see what we have that will fit." She had been warned by Tommy Smith about Margaret's horror of receiving charity. "I hope I have picked out frocks you will like, Margaret."

"And a coat?" Sarah asked anxiously.

"And some coats," Miss Grey agreed, "and, anyway, even if you don't like the clothes, dressing up is always fun, isn't it?"

40

Alone on the stage, Sir John clasped Tommy's hand.

"It was the laugh that settled it. Anyone who can laugh like that on a partly lit stage wearing an old jersey and skirt—"

"And black boots," Tommy reminded him.

"And black boots," Sir John agreed, "has the makings of a fine actress."

Upstairs in Katie's bedroom, six frocks and three coats and some hats were awaiting Margaret's approval. But first Miss Grey introduced the two girls to each other.

"Did Papa give you the part?" Katie asked, and when Margaret nodded, she turned proudly to Miss Grey. "I told you he would. I heard him singing in his bath, and he only does that when he's found a new actor or actress for his company."

"What are you doing about lessons?" Miss Grey asked.

It was Sarah who answered.

"We shall have to move. We're staying with my sister near Drury Lane, but it's a small room and she's stout, and I'm not what you'd call willowy, so we'll have to move on, and then Margaret'll go to the school that's nearest."

"Are there a lot of children in the play?" Miss Grey asked.

"No," said Margaret. "I suppose I'll have an understudy."

Katie broke in. "In the cathedral scene at the end there are children, choirboys, and little grand dukes and duchesses, people like that."

Margaret was surprised.

"Then you've read the play?"

The girls had moved away from Miss Grey and Sarah.

"I read them all," Katie whispered. "Uncle Tommy lends them to me. This play, of course, I read and reread because Papa wanted me to be Anastasia, but Mama would not let me. She doesn't want me to be an actress. But I will be someday."

"Have you ever acted?" Margaret asked.

"When I was eight I did. It was for charity. Papa put on *A Midsummer Night's Dream*. I was Puck. It was lovely."

Miss Grey glanced at the two girls.

"I don't know if it will be possible, but I will try to arrange that Margaret does lessons with Katie. Katie needs another child to work with, and it will be convenient when rehearsals start, for I can fit her in when she is free."

Triumphantly Sarah and Margaret, with all the frocks and coats and hats, went home in a taxi.

"Imagine Sir John paying me two pounds a week just to look after you!" said Sarah.

"Now that we know I'm going to earn four pounds a week, would you lend me enough money to buy some shoes?" Margaret asked.

"Of course, dear," Sarah agreed. "A pity your feet were bigger than Miss Katie's."

Margaret looked at her feet.

"I do despise boots," she said.

7. The Calendar

It was Lou who found accommodations for Sarah and Margaret.

"My room's all right for me," she said, "and it's handy for the theater and all that, but it's on the rough side around here. What you and Margaret want is a couple of rooms and a kitchen in a more select neighborhood."

It was not easy to find rooms in what Lou meant by a more select neighborhood, because people in select neighborhoods did not let off rooms in their houses; it was not considered genteel. However, by a bit of luck, Lou heard of rooms that sounded just what they wanted, and she could not get home quickly enough to tell Sarah the news.

"It was Miss Violet de Lang," she explained, "second boy she is in our panto. I was fitting her gold tunic for our all-gold finale when she happened to tell me where she was staying. It's in an ever so nice square not far from here. Seems her auntie was cook to a lady and her husband was odd-job man, and when the lady died, having no relatives, she left the house and all in it to Miss de Lang's auntie. But it's too big for her and her hubby, so they want a nice quiet let. Well, when I told Miss de Lang about you and Margaret, she said you sounded just what her auntie was looking for."

The next day Sarah and Margaret went around to see Miss de Lang's auntie. They combined the visit with going to a shoe shop for Margaret's shoes. For the occasion Margaret wore some of her new clothes, and very nice she looked. Both Sarah and Lou were most impressed when she was dressed.

"Might be anybody," said Lou.

Margaret did not fancy her position in the world being judged by her clothes, so up went her chin into the air.

"Well, I might be anybody. I've told you how I was found in a basket. . . ."

Lou was tired of hearing that story, which, in any case, she did not believe.

"I know, with three of everything of the very best quality. But I'll tell you this, my girl, there's some who pay for dressing and some who don't. Well, you do and you should remember to say thank you to God in your prayers."

The shoe shop Lou recommended was very grand—too grand for Sarah, who, when asked by one of the assistants what she wanted, could only whisper "shoes," not saying who they were for. But Margaret was not put off by grandeur.

"It's shoes for me," she told the assistant. "I want shoes for walking and another pair for the house."

When they sat down to try on shoes, the assistant, unlacing Margaret's boots, found it hard to hide her surprise that such a beautifully dressed little girl should be wearing not only old clumsy boots but thick, coarse black stockings. However, she said nothing but carefully fitted

Margaret out in black-laced shoes and a pair of soft house shoes. Then she said to Sarah, "Would you care to see some stockings? These the little girl is wearing are thicker than we recommend with our shoes."

Sarah thought stockings were stockings and that was that, but Margaret jumped at the idea.

"What do you recommend?" she asked. "And please throw away the boots. I don't want them anymore."

Sarah was appalled. Throw away boots! She had never heard of such extravagance. The shock of the suggestion brought back her voice.

"Please pack the boots. We do not know when they may be needed. And we do not require stockings."

The room proved to be just what was wanted, and Mrs. Wallow, Miss de Lang's auntie, immediately put Sarah at her ease. She was a thin little woman, dressed in black with a neat lace cap on her head.

"I'll just show you the rooms," she said, "and then perhaps you'll have a cup of tea. It will be in the kitchen, for it's what I'm used to, never having sat in a drawing room and I'm not starting now. It's just two bedrooms you can have. I can't give you a kitchen, but you can share mine or, if convenient, I could cook for us all, being used to it, like. But I tell you what you can use, and that is the bathroom. Mr. Wallow and I have ours by the kitchen stove of a Saturday night as we've always done, but no doubt you'd fancy the bathroom."

The rooms were small but clean, with flowered wallpaper and dark green curtains and bed coverings. Both had texts over the bed. Sarah had "God is Love" and Margaret "Thou God see'st me." Neither Sarah nor Margaret

45

had ever before lived where there was a bathroom. They thought it superb.

"When he has the time," Mrs. Wallow said, "Mr. Wallow will do up the big front bedroom for a sitting room, but there's no saying when he can get around to it, for he keeps funny hours, being an odd-job man."

Over tea in the kitchen Mrs. Wallow heard about The Dolphin Theater. She said her niece had told her the little girl was a theatrical but she had not known she was to appear at The Dolphin. Then she added, "But I knew she was someone special as soon as I opened the door. You can't mistake good clothes when you see them."

Sarah, just to be friendly, was about to tell Mrs. Wallow about Margaret's luck on being given Miss Katie's cast-off clothes when Margaret gave her such a look that she hurriedly shut her mouth. She knew she was already in disgrace for having refused to throw away the boots or lend the money for finer stockings for, since leaving the shoe shop, Margaret had stumped along, refusing to say a word. So instead of telling Mrs. Wallow about Katie's clothes, she turned the conversation to business—the all-important question of rent and when they could move in.

While this was going on Margaret wandered around the exquisitely kept kitchen. Suddenly she came face-to-face with a calendar. It had a picture on it of the countryside in autumn. In the foreground there was a field so like the one in which the Fortescues had set up their theater that Margaret felt she was there. She could almost see the little tent Sarah had used for the wardrobe. Looking at it again in her mind's eye, it was as if a wind blew through Margaret, for suddenly she was breathless with love for Sarah and bitterly ashamed of herself. Sarah had

46

not wanted to run away. She was happy with the Fortescues. She had done it for her. But for Sarah and her savings. Margaret would never have heard of The Dolphin Theater. But for Sarah she would never have bought those gorgeous shoes. She had been an ungrateful beast. However hard she tried, she could never thank Sarah enough.

Just then Sarah got up and said good-bye to Mrs. Wallow, and told her to expect them the following afternoon.

Margaret also said good bye to Mrs. Wallow, but directly they were in the street, she slipped a hand under Sarah's arm and squeezed it.

"I do love you, Sarah, truly I do. I don't want to be a beast like I was this morning, and I do pray I never will be again, but if I am, please scold me, for I'm afraid I have a difficult nature."

8.   Miss Grey Has a Plan

Miss Grey was not by nature timorous. It was impossible to be timorous, brought up as she had been, for in those days just living had been an adventure. Her father had been an extremely honest man and would not only have been appalled if he had known any of the food on his table was not honestly come by but would have refused to eat it. So if sometimes fish had come from rivers they had no right to fish in, or a pheasant was caught in a rabbit snare, she had been as skilled as her sisters in explaining the unexplainable. This gift, however, did not help her in dealing with Lady Teaser, of whom she was terrified. Though Lady Teaser had never called her "that comical Miss Grey" to her face, she made it perfectly clear that was how she thought of her. If she had arranged things, Miss Grey would never have come inside her home, but Sir John had arranged everything.

"Katie doesn't want a real governess. She can go to all the classes she requires. What she needs is a friend. She is much too quiet for a child of her age. She wants someone to laugh and play with."

Except for her fear of Lady Teaser, Miss Grey would have been utterly happy with Katie. She had nothing to do, of course, with The Dolphin Theater, for their apartments had even a separate entrance. But, through Katie, she was in touch with the theater, and best of all she saw plays, for Sir John had given her permission to ask for a theater seat for all his productions and told the manager, Tommy Smith, to get her seats on her day off for any other theaters she might wish to see. And at Christmas seats were booked for Katie and herself at pantomimes and for the musical shows that were all the fashion, but best of all, there was Shakespeare. Miss Grey had no idea why she was so fond of the theater, for she had no wish to act herself and had no dreams of becoming a playwright. She was just theater-mad and there was no explaining it.

However, though she had applied for the position of governess to Katie because it would bring her in touch with the theater, that did not mean she did not take her work seriously. She had come to Katie when the child was eight and from the beginning had been devoted to her. She had arrived just when Katie's Nannie, because of illness, had left her and Katie was rehearsing Puck for the charity performances of *A Midsummer Night's Dream*, a difficult time for an eight-year-old. Miss Grey had been exactly the person Katie had needed; in her own way just as engrossed in the play as Katie, prepared at any moment to be Oberon, Titania, or any other character with whom Katie spoke; willing to discuss indefinitely the spirit of Puck; able to help the child bear the attitude of her mother when it was suggested by her father, since she had been such a success as Puck, that Katie should have some stage training.

Now, though she knew if she had her way and Lady

49

Teaser heard it was her idea, she would probably be dismissed. She felt she must fight for Katie's right to have someone with whom she could do lessons and with whom she could be friends, so she sent a note to Tommy Smith.

"Dear Mr. Smith. Could you arrange that I have a few minutes' talk with Sir John? Yours respectfully, Selina Grey."

Tommy passed on the message to Sir John, who looked anxious.

"What does she want? I thought everything was working happily in the schoolroom."

"So it is," said Tommy. "I expect it's to do with the clothes for Margaret Thursday. Could you see her after luncheon?"

Miss Grey, dressed as always in a coat and skirt with a shirt blouse, her clod-hopping shoes just showing under her skirt, tapped on Sir John's door. Sir John rose to greet her and pulled out a chair for her.

"Something wrong? Katie in disgrace?"

This was a joke, for Katie was never in disgrace, so Miss Grey smiled and ignored it.

"I allowed Katie to help me fit Margaret Thursday out in her clothes. The girls took to each other. It came to me that perhaps it could be arranged that I teach Margaret during rehearsals. Katie would love it, and it would be a convenience to you, for I could teach the child when she could be spared."

Sir John did not answer at once. Then he said, "I doubt her Ladyship would agree. You know how she feels about the theater."

Miss Grey nodded.

"Naturally I know. But I also know that Katie knows all

50

about *The Little Queen.* The servants told her. I believe there was hope in the kitchen that Katie might play the part, a hope Katie has undoubtedly shared. Besides being a convenience to you, it would be a consolation to Katie to have the fun of working with another child."

Sir John considered this.

"It would be a great convenience to me. These new education laws and licenses are a terrible nuisance. Children did capitally without them—look at Ellen Terry. I'll have to wait until her Ladyship is in the right mood and then I will put forward your suggestion. Thank you for making it, Miss Grey."

Sarah and Margaret moved into their rooms at Mrs. Wallow's, and Margaret at once wrote to The Dolphin, giving Mr. Smith her change of address.

"Do you think we had better find a school for me?" she asked Sarah.

Sarah felt, now Margaret was engaged to play at The Dolphin Theater, that such matters as schools were for Sir John and Mr. Smith to decide.

"Leave it until rehearsals start," she advised. "There must be arrangements for schooling for theatrical children, and Lou says you have to have a license. I expect they'll see about that."

Margaret was sure Sarah was right, but she thought life in a genteel neighborhood terribly dull. It had been much more exciting when they stayed with Lou, for there was always something going on in the streets, even if it was only a fight. Then there was the fun of supper when Lou came home brimful of theater gossip and descriptions of the clothes she was making. Now nothing happened; they

51

did not even go shopping, for it had been so much easier to allow Mrs. Wallow to cook for them, and it made such a change from their own small rooms to go down to the kitchen for meals.

Then, just as Margaret, who was never good at being bored, decided she could not endure going on as they were a day longer, a note was delivered from The Dolphin Theater. It said, "Lady Teaser wishes to see you. Will you please come to the theater at three o'clock on Friday next."

Friday was two days away.

9. Her Ladyship Hears the Story

Although she no longer acted, Lady Teaser liked to know what was going on in their theater. So when Sir John asked her if she would allow the little girl he hoped would play Anastasia to do lessons with Katie during the rehearsal period, she decided it was a good chance to have a look at the child. She did not suppose she would allow the girl anywhere near Katie, for probably under the veneer of breeding taught to all young actresses she was a common little thing. However, the excuse that she was just seeing Margaret Thursday as a possible playmate for Katie was a good one, so she told Sir John, if he sent for the girl, that she would see her.

In an old-fashioned way Margaret had been well brought up. So when she was shown into Lady Teaser's drawing room, she gave a bob curtsy and said politely, "Good afternoon."

Lady Teaser noted with amusement how well Katie's coat suited Margaret, but she also noticed that it had been beautifully altered.

"Good afternoon," she said. Then she pointed to a chair. "You may sit, or is the coat too tight to sit down in?"

Margaret sat.

"It was tight to begin with, but Sarah—who I live with— she's let it out and now it is lovely and comfortable. I wish Hannah, who brought me up, could see me now. She wished she could send me to the orphanage with nice clothes, but we had to wear uniforms there. It was wicked what we looked like. These are the first nice clothes I ever had."

Lady Teaser gave a gracious nod, accepting Margaret's unspoken thanks.

"Is it true you were found in a basket?"

Margaret was delighted to find a new audience. She was careful this time not to embellish the story as she often did, adding coronets on her baby clothes, for there was a look in Lady Teaser's eyes that made Margaret feel that she would notice any exaggeration.

"It was the rector really who found me. It was on the church steps and he got the two old ladies, Miss Sylvia and Miss Selina Cameron, to adopt me and arranged that Hannah would look after me, but they got old and the fifty-two pounds a year, which had always come for my keep, stopped coming."

"So you were sent to an orphanage?"

"Yes. The Archdeacon had a brother who was a gover- nor of one. I was sent there, but it was more terrible than you could dream it would be, so I and the boys ran away."

Lady Teaser raised her eyebrows.

"Boys! What boys?"

"Well, at first they were just orphans like me, we hid on a canal boat and—"

Lady Teaser held up a hand.

54

"Do not gabble, child. Who were the boys?"

"Well, they were Lavinia's brothers, Peter and Horatio Beresford. The boys were in the orphanage like me, but Lavinia was fourteen, so she was found a place in Lady Corkberry's kitchen."

Lady Teaser was a great reader of social gossip columns, so she knew where the Corkberrys' stately home was.

"At Sedgecombe Place?"

"That's it, so when the boys and I ran away from the orphanage, that's where we went, for I thought we'd find Lavinia and she would know where to hide the boys."

"Why did you want to hide the boys?"

Margaret, when telling people her history, usually left out the part about the elder of the two boys, Peter, but now she had to explain.

"We'd been to tea with the Archdeacon's brother, the one who got me into the orphanage, and we were driven over to tea in one of the Corkberry traps. I sat in front, which was how I got to know Jem, because he was driving the trap. It was his father who had a canal boat, so when we escaped from the orphanage, Jem took us to his mother. Ma Smith she is called."

"And you hid on the canal boat. But why?"

"Well, Peter had borrowed books from the Archdeacon's brother without telling him, and we were afraid he might have thought they were stolen and tell the police. That's why we had to run away, but I'd meant to, anyway. The orphanage was truly terrible."

"Why did you leave the canal boat?"

"The work was very hard. You see, we were leggers." Margaret saw that Lady Teaser did not know what the

55

term meant. "You know how canal boats are pulled by horses? Well, we led the horses, cruel hard work it was in wet weather and Peter fainted, so Mrs. Smith put him to bed and said we couldn't go on being leggers."

"So what did you do then?"

"Mrs. Smith had a sister called Ida, who called herself Mrs. Fortescue, but it wasn't their real name. She and Mr. Fortescue had a fit-up company that played in a tent all the summer, and we were put to work for them. It was meant Peter should be Lord Fauntleroy, but he couldn't act, so instead I was Lord Fauntleroy, and Horatio, he was the little boy, acted the wrong Lord Fauntleroy."

"And where are the boys now?"

"Oh, their grandfather, only they didn't know they had one, came for them and took them all to Ireland where he has a castle."

"A castle! What is his name?"

"The Marquis of Delaware. Their mother, who died, had been Lady Phoebe Delaware. Lavinia looked like her mother and Lord Corkberry guessed who she was and went to Ireland to tell Lord Delaware he had found her."

Lady Teaser managed to hide her delight, but it was difficult. She had always said that Katie was not to be an actress but should be brought up to be a fashionable young lady, but she had never been sure how she could do it, and now, through this most unlikely source, she could see a way.

"Do you ever hear from the children now?"

"I had one letter from Lavinia, but I haven't answered it yet. I wanted an address to give her. Lord Delaware wanted me to go to Ireland too. He wanted to adopt me. But I wouldn't go. He said if I'd go, he would treat me as a daughter. But I don't want to be treated as anybody's daughter. I'm Margaret Thursday and I'm going to make my name famous."

Lady Teaser got to her feet.

"I'm sure you will, dear. Now come up to the school-room and make friends with Katie. I hope you two will do lessons together and become great friends."

The stage-door keeper at The Dolphin was a well-known figure in his own right. To his inferiors—such as window cleaners, inexperienced dressers, tradespeople who delivered at the stage door, and any persons he did not accept as his equal—he was known as Mr. Todd. To the actors and countless others he was just Bill. Sometimes, when he could step out to have a glass of port, a friend full of good spirits might slap him on the back and call him Toddie. When this happened, he would say quietly, "The name is Bill." No one ever argued with this.

Sarah had been left at the stage door while Margaret was up with Lady Teaser, so Bill had to think what would be best to do with her. He had what was called "his room" at the stage door, but it was little more than a box with no room for a second chair, but there was a packing case on which he could sit, so he opened his door and invited her in.

"I'm afraid I don't know your name, ma'am, but if you'd care to sit down while waiting for the little girl, I would be pleased."

Sarah was also pleased, so she stepped in and sat.

As Bill always said of himself, he had a rare nose for picking out who was who. Even as Sarah was sitting down, he knew Margaret was not related to her. A nice, good woman he was sure, and certainly a theatrical, but as different from the little girl as chalk from cheese. On a ledge in the corner of his box Bill had a gas burner on which he could do a little cooking or boil a kettle. Now he got up and lit it.

"I expect you could do with a cup of tea. There's a nip in the air, which is, I suppose, only natural with winter coming on. Soon we'll be havin' fogs. I can't abide the dirty things. A real pea-souper clears the theater like a dose of salts."

"I know," Sarah agreed. "But I've been working outside London recently and though, of course, fogs do come up, they aren't the terror they are in London."

"I'm glad to hear the guv'nor is giving the part to little Miss Thursday. This play what's running here is finishing, so we ought to start rehearsals for the new one if we are to be settled in before Christmas. Could be quite a holiday attraction with a little girl playing the queen."

"And what a little girl!" said Sarah proudly. "Why, the moment she stepped on the stage as Little Lord Fauntleroy, we all knew. Real find she is."

"Where was she found, ma'am?" Bill asked.

Sarah waited while Bill heated the teapot.

"On a Thursday in a basket on the steps of the church. With the baby was a wardrobe of three of everything all of the very best quality. There was a note with her that said, "This is Margaret, whom I entrust to your care. Each year fifty-two pounds will be sent for her keep and schooling. She has not yet been christened.'"

Bill stared at Sarah.

"Is that the truth? You aren't 'avin' me on?"

"It's the truth," said Sarah. "And it seems, up to this

year, the money always came, but this year there was only a card on which was printed: "No more money for Margaret.' "

Bill made the tea and handed a cup to Sarah, offering at the same time milk and sugar.

"Is that how she came to be on the boards?"

"Oh, no. There was, it seems, the rector of the church in charge of her, though she was brought up by two old ladies. No, she joined the Fortescue Comedy Company, which is a fit-up where I worked, by accident, like. As there was no more money for her keep, this rector sent her to an orphanage. Of course, we all know there's bad orphanages around, but from what Margaret says, the one the rector chose was just about as bad as it could be. So Margaret ups and runs away, taking two little boys along with her. They joins one of those canal boats as leggers, which it seems is what they call those that lead the horses."

Bill felt Sarah was being too gullible.

"Do you believe all what she says?"

"Oh, yes. You see, the boys was not suited to the legging, and the barge people asked Mrs. Fortescue—sister she is to the barge owner—to take the boys to be actors. Well, we wanted a clever boy to play Little Lord Fauntleroy, but Peter, the elder of the two boys, just could not act at all."

"There are some like that," Bill agreed.

"Yes," said Sarah, "so Mr. Fortescue lost patience and threatened to beat him, and that's when Margaret rushes in and in a flash they sees where the talent is. So Margaret's in and Peter's out. Not that it mattered to the boys, for their grandfather comes for them, by all accounts he—"

Bill put up a hand to stop Sarah.

"Don't tell me. He's a lord and the boy was the missing heir."

Sarah laughed.

"Truth is often stranger than fiction."

"I'll say," Bill agreed, "but this Margaret's story is enough to be goin' on with. Found in a basket, sent to an orphanage, escapes on a canal boat, and finishes in a theater. Stone the crows, but I believe you, though thousands wouldn't."

"It's all true," said Sarah, "but, mind you, I think that's just the beginning of her story. You wait until this play comes on. I've a feeling in my bones somebody is going to recognize her."

10. Lessons

Rehearsals began ten days later, and before they started, Sarah brought Margaret daily to The Dolphin for her lessons. The Teasers lived in a style Lady Teaser considered to befit their position. She had her personal maid, and Sir John his valet, who was also his theater dresser. There was a butler and a footman called Henry with a parlormaid to work with him. In the kitchen there was Mrs. Melly, the cook, who was famous in theatrical London for her cooking. She was waited upon by two kitchen maids.

The place was spacious. There was a vast drawing room and almost as large a dining room, a sitting room for Sir John, and a morning room for Lady Teaser. Katie had a sitting room, which every morning was converted by Henry into a schoolroom. To do this he carried in a sturdy schoolroom table and put on it a large globe of the world and an armful of schoolbooks.

Neither Katie nor Miss Grey by as much as an exchanged look admitted that they were accepting a farce. There was no need to bring in a schoolroom table. There was a pretty writing desk Katie could have used. The globe looked handsome and was what you would expect to find in a schoolroom, but it was never used as part of a geography lesson. Instead it was the door to adventure. At any moment either Miss Grey or Katie would spin it, and both would wait breathlessly to see where it stopped, then Miss Grey would say, "Oh, what fun, this morning, we are in Russia. . . ." Peking, Malta, it did not matter where, so long as they had reference books and could read about where they were visiting.

The same kind of pretending went on about the piano. There was a nice little upright piano in Katie's sitting room, and each day she had to practice on it to be ready for her music lessons on Tuesdays and Fridays. Miss Grey had never learned to play the piano and could not read a note of music, but every day Henry had to bring in a stool and place it by the piano for Miss Grey to sit on while she "supervised" the piano practice.

Both Katie and Miss Grey were full of excitement the day Margaret started lessons. Now there was purpose in the schoolroom table. It was needed, for two girls could not use the desk.

Sharp at nine o'clock, Henry knocked on the schoolroom door.

"It's the little girl, Miss Katie."

Margaret thought that a poor introduction. She swept past Henry and said, "Me and Mrs. Beamish." Then she looked at Katie. "Oh, you are wearing a pinafore. Sarah said you would. I've got two. I'll wear one tomorrow."

That first morning Miss Grey set Margaret a kind of examination, so she could see how much she knew. This proved that at ordinary lessons, like sums and geography, Margaret was well ahead of Katie, but at reading books, poetry, or plays, Katie was far in advance of Margaret.

While the girls were working, Sarah and Miss Grey discussed plans.

"What time will you be through with Margaret?" Sarah asked.

Miss Grey thought about that.

"I take Katie for a walk at twelve, then, after our dinner, she goes to a class. It's dancing today, I think Margaret may as well come too."

Sarah was more down-to-earth than Miss Grey.

"Lessons like that cost money."

"These won't," Miss Grey promised. "Most of the teachers we use have worked for Sir John at some time and, though, of course he pays for Katie, they'll take Margaret free. After all, it's only until rehearsals start. She couldn't go after that."

Sarah nodded.

"So I'll pick Margaret up about five?"

"Five or six. After tea they can play together. Katie's got a lovely dollhouse."

"I don't know that Margaret's much of a one for dolls," said Sarah, "but they'll be happy together, I've no doubt. And her being here will suit me a treat, for it will give me a chance to see my sister Lou."

Those days before the rehearsals started were very happy ones for both girls. Katie had never mixed much with other children and Margaret, though she had been to school, had always been hurried home by Hannah, who had to get the old ladies' tea, so she had never made a school friend. At the orphanage she had known other children, but talking was discouraged. As a result, when Katie and Margaret were together, it was as if dams broke in each of them and conversation came pouring out.

"If you two talk instead of eating," said Miss Grey, "I shall have to make a rule: no talking at meals."

Of course, Katie was thrilled to hear about Margaret's life, for she thought, compared to her own, that it was breathtakingly exciting. She was particularly interested in the boys who had run away from the orphanage with Margaret.

"You ought to meet Peter," said Margaret. "He was always reading. He never could get enough books. That's how he came to borrow three: *Bleak House, Ivanhoe,* and *Kenilworth.*"

Katie could imagine poor Peter starved of anything to read.

"I've read those. I don't wonder Peter borrowed them. They are all very good."

"He's got all he wants to read now. I had a letter from Lavinia, and she says Peter can have all the books he likes. There is a big library, but as well his grandfather orders books from Dublin."

"What else did she say?"

"They have a governess and a tutor to teach them, and they've all got ponies to ride."

"I wish they didn't live so far away," said Katie. "I would love to meet them. It would be like having a family."

Margaret nodded.

"Lord Delaware asked me to go to Ireland. He said he would bring me up as a daughter, but I don't need anyone to bring me up, for I have a mother of my own."

"Have you told Lavinia that you are going to act in a production at The Dolphin?"

Margaret looked a little ashamed.

"I haven't answered her yet. You see, I don't write letters much. I've nobody to write to."

Katie understood.

"Miss Grey gives me lessons on letter writing." She lowered her voice. "She doesn't know much about writing them, either, but Mama said I had to learn, as it is part of a lady's task. So she bought a book on etiquette and that is full of letters and the right way to address people. You know, when to say 'Esteemed Sir' and when to say 'Dear Sir.' Anyway you don't want anything like that to write to Lavinia. Let's send her a letter tomorrow."

Helped by Katie, Margaret wrote a splendid letter to Lavinia, telling her all about Sarah and their lodgings and, of course, "Katie says you will see in the newspapers when *The Little Queen* begins. It would be wonderful if you could come to London to see me in it. My love to you all, Margaret."

"Do you think she really might come?" Katie asked.

Margaret was incapable of imagining her friend Lavinia's life in Ireland. When she had known her, she had been a kitchen maid. Now she lived in a castle, and there was a governess, a tutor, and ponies. However, she was not going to admit that she did not know.

"I expect so. One day, without anything being said, there'll be a knock on my dressing-room door and there she'll be."

11. Rehearsal

Rehearsal was called for eleven o'clock. For this first day it was to be a reading of the play, but though it was only a reading, Margaret was in such a state of nerves that poor Sarah found it hard not to become impatient. First Margaret argued about what she should wear.

"But you chose the pink yourself, dear. You said it was ever so pretty—which it is—so I ironed it special."

"But you haven't given me my lace underclothes. It isn't Sunday, but I'm sure Hannah would think it was a day for lace."

That made Sarah cross.

"Everything put in your chest of drawers is washed and ironed and ready to wear. You can't say different. Put on your lace if you feel like it."

That made Margaret ashamed. Sarah kept her clothes beautifully, and she knew she was being horrid but somehow she couldn't stop.

"Well, I think you might have guessed it would be a lace day."

Sarah bit back what she felt like saying and walked out of the room.

It had been arranged by Sarah that Margaret should

66

come down to breakfast in her old skirt and jersey so there would be no risk of marking her frock. Now, as she started to put them on, Margaret felt a revulsion against them. Would Sarah understand why she wouldn't put them on? She went to Sarah's room and knocked on the door. Sarah thought she had come to apologize, so she gave Margaret a kiss.

"It's all right, dear, it's only natural that you should feel in a state, meeting all the other actresses and actors for the first time."

Margaret returned Sarah's kiss, but then she held out the jersey and skirt.

"I can't wear these, even though you've washed them. I always remember that that awful Matron at the orphanage touched them and I think they smell of her, and I feel it would be unlucky to wear them today."

Sarah had, of course, heard all about the orphanage, but she had never quite understood Margaret's detestation of the place.

"Well, put on one of your pinnies, that'll keep you clean. But you know, dear, it doesn't do to brood on what's behind you. I daresay it seemed terrible in that orphanage at the time, but if you were to go there now, I expect you'd find it was not one half as bad as you remember."

"I'd find it worse than I remember," said Margaret. "Much, much worse."

Tommy Smith introduced Margaret to the cast.

"Can you manage a curtsy?" he asked her. "Not deep, just a bob."

"I can. But do I have to?"

Tommy Smith's eyes twinkled.

"You don't have to, but it will be thought very good manners if you do."

"Then I will," said Margaret. "As long as they know it's not because I feel inferior, because I don't."

The actors were chatting on the stage. Tommy led Margaret to each group.

"This is Margaret Thursday," he explained, "who plays the child queen."

Then he named each actor in turn who, by a nod or a smile, greeted her. In return she gave to each a polite bob curtsy. No one paid much attention to her, for that children should be seen but not heard was practiced in the theater as in the home. But though Margaret did not know it, a few approving remarks were passed. "Quite a nice-looking child." "If the child acts as well as she looks, she will pass."

Margaret did not tell Tommy Smith that she was offended but bottled her feelings up to pour them onto Sarah, but she was frustrated, for another child was sitting beside Sarah. It was expected that child actresses would have some adult in charge of them. Margaret's understudy, who had been called to the play reading, had no adult with her; she was one of a family of nine and there was nobody to take her to the theater. Her overworked mother had said, "You go on your own and sit down by whoever's lookin' after the other child. Nobody can't complain of that." Then she gave her a small parcel. "And there's your bite to eat dinnertime."

Sarah quite happily accepted the understudy.

"And what's your name, dear?"

The child was dressed in a near-black satin coat and a black velvet hat, for black satin was the favorite wear for little girl actresses. She now smoothed out the skirt of her coat.

"Eliza Wigan. D'you like my coat? My ma made it, though she had to pawn her own coat and my old one to get the stuff."

Sarah honestly did admire it, for she considered black satin, even near-black satin, smart.

"Very nice it is. Is this your first engagement?"

Liza laughed.

"No, I was first on when I was three, danced and sang and did the splits and that, in the public 'ouses. From there I went to the 'alls. Baby Liza they called me. Then I was in panto. I never got on as far as I might, 'cause we never 'ad no money for lessons. You see, there's nine of us. I'm the eldest, I'm eleven."

Sarah quite understood. The story was not unlike her own.

"I didn't start so young as you, but I couldn't have lessons, either. You see, my mother was a widow and, when my father was took, was left with the nine of us. She earned just enough to keep us with her needle. Lovely needlewoman she was, and she taught all us girls to needle too. Then one day, when I was twelve and my sister Lou was fourteen, we got the chance to go into a pantomime. We never went 'ome after that, for when we couldn't get work in the theater, there was always sewin' to be had. I did quite well. There was seldom a week when I didn't send something home to my ma."

Margaret, seeing Sarah and Liza deep in conversation, realized it was not the moment to tell Sarah what she felt about the cast.

"There you are, dear," Sarah said. "This is the understudy, Liza Wigan. Liza, this is Margaret Thursday."

The two girls stared at each other. They looked very different: Margaret, simply but well dressed in a warm, soft dull pink dress, and Liza, all ringlets and black satin, but that was only outside. Inside, they were not so unlike, and they both felt it. As it happened, they had barely greeted each other when the reading started. Tommy Smith called out, "Please sit, everybody, and have your pencils ready to mark the cuts." Then he added: "Come over here, Margaret, and sit in the front where you can hear what is going on."

No sooner were all the cast seated with their scripts open at Act I than Sir John came onto the stage. He made quite an entrance. The gaslights were turned up so it felt as if he brought light with him. He stood for a moment where everybody could see him. Then he bowed.

"Good morning, everybody. Now, if you are ready, we will start."

A large chair had been put ready for him, and he sank gracefully into it.

Then it was Tommy Smith's turn. He said loudly and clearly, "*The Little Queen.* Act One, Scene One. The library at Souton Hall."

12. Licenses

On the whole Margaret found rehearsals a bore. She enjoyed her own scenes enormously, especially her favorite, where she lost her temper, but there seemed to be so much of the play when she was not on the stage. During those scenes she was supposed to do lessons. They were set by Miss Grey and were usually very simple, for she did not see how Margaret could study and keep one ear open so that she did not miss her entrance.

One afternoon when Katie was having a music lesson, Miss Grey took Margaret and Liza to the magistrate's court to get licenses permitting them to appear at The Dolphin. To Liza it was a great day, for they drove to the magistrate's court. They traveled in what was called a growler, a four-wheeled horse-drawn conveyance. Miss Grey smiled to herself as she watched Liza grandly allowing Mr. Todd to help her into the cab.

The magistrate was not fierce, as Miss Grey had feared he might be. He asked Margaret a few simple questions, but the fact that she had a governess was all that he seemed to need to know. Miss Grey let Liza answer for herself, for she had no idea who was educating her or where they did it—if indeed she was educated at all.

"I'm only the understudy, your Worship," said Liza, grinning at him from under her cheap velvet hat, "so I goes to school regular. You see, I don't 'ave to wait in the theater till the play's over, so I don't need to sleep in, for if Margaret's fine, I can go 'ome when the curtain's down on the first act.'

"Who takes you home?" the magistrate asked.

Sounding a little shocked, Liza replied primly, "Me Ma, of course. She won't have any of us out on the streets of a night time."

"Quite right," said the magistrate, and both children received their licenses.

In the cab driving back to The Dolphin, Miss Grey asked Liza how, with so many babies at home, her mother found time to collect her from the theater. Liza gave her a wink.

" 'Course she don't fetch me, nor I wouldn't want her to. I been getting around on my own since I was five. But if it does the old geezer good to think I'm fetched, why spoil his fun?"

During rehearsals Margaret had to go to the wardrobe for fittings of her ordinary stage clothes. For Anastasia's coronation robes, Sarah had to take her to somebody called a court dressmaker, who made, so it was said, dresses for Queen Victoria. Margaret did not think this much of a recommendation, for in all the pictures she had seen of the Queen, she had worn dull black dresses just like any ordinary old lady would wear. Whatever they might have made for Queen Victoria, the dressmakers had let themselves go over Anastasia's coronation clothes: velvet and satin sewn all over with what looked like diamonds and pearls and a great train edged with fur.

"Won't I look beautiful!" Margaret had gasped to Sarah the first time she had tried the dress on.

Sarah did not hold with that kind of talk.

"Pride comes before a fall," she said, and "Beauty is as beauty does."

But Margaret did not care what anybody said. She thought she knew why the dress felt so right.

"I think if I knew who I was, this is the kind of dress I would wear every day, even for breakfast."

It was during the third week of rehearsals that trouble blew up for Margaret. By then she knew the part perfectly and, since rehearsals had gone well, was feeling confident—perhaps too confident. Suddenly, in the middle of the scene in the hotel on the frontier of Parthenia, Sir John stopped the rehearsal. It was Margaret's least favorite scene, the one she thought rather mushy, where her father told her how beautifully people in high positions should behave. Margaret was more or less listening, but a part of her mind was wondering how long it would be before she had an answer to her letter to Lavinia. Sir John stopped in the middle of a sentence and he sounded really angry.

"You are not in the scene."

Margaret was mortified. It was not nice being scolded in front of all the cast. She sounded a little cross.

"I'm sorry, Sir John, but I don't know what you mean."

"You weren't listening to me. Part of your mind was somewhere else. You must listen to what is said when you are on the stage or the scene drops dead. Now, we'll start that scene again and this time listen. Listen, listen. . . ."

It is very difficult to listen to words you know perfectly

well. That time Margaret truly tried, but still Sir John was not pleased.

"You may be listening now. I think you think you are. But I don't believe the audience will know you are. An actor must show he is listening. He must react."

Finally they finished with that scene and went on with the rest of the act. Sir John did not criticize her again, and Margaret had no further trouble. But inside she was worried because she knew what Sir John had said was true; she had been only partly listening. It was something new about acting, and she had an uncomfortable feeling that it was something she did not quite understand.

They had seldom rehearsed the last scene, for it was almost entirely pageantry and music, but two weeks before the play opened, the cast was told that much of the next week would be spent on the last act. This meant that several more children came to rehearsals. The one who had the most to do was called Simon; he was a page. He was a terribly thin little boy who did not seem to want to mix with the other children. Margaret tried to talk to him because he reminded her of Peter, Lavinia's brother, who had escaped with her on the canal boat, but she did not have much success because he seemed scared to talk and only said yes or no.

Liza, her eyes twinkling, watched Margaret's efforts.

"It won't do no good, he's scared to talk. He's one of Ma Mud's kids. That's not her real name, but it's what we call her."

"Who is she?"

"No one knows, turns up with two or three kids, or-phans she says they are, and starts them earning money for her. Simon and one or two others she fixes in the theater, but mostly they goes in the sweatshops."

"What are they?"

"Where smart clothes is made. They aren't allowed to use little kids no more, but she gets by with it. She can smell a copper a mile away, Ma Mud can."

"Poor Simon looks terribly thin. Do you think she gives them enough to eat?"

Liza shook her head.

"No one knows for certain sure, but it's said she feeds 'em dead cats and rats!"

Margaret shuddered.

"Sounds like the Matron of that orphanage I was in. She didn't give us cats and rats, but she would have if she dared."

After that talk, Margaret, with the help of Katie, gave Simon little treats: a piece of chocolate, a slice of cake, and once at dinner, when Miss Grey was not looking, they made him a meat sandwich.

"Poor Simon, we can help now when we see him all day, but it won't be so easy when the play starts."

"You leave it to me," said Liza. "I'll find a way to give 'im what you get. That Ma Mud 'angs out in the street next to ours. . . . When I sees 'er comin', I crosses over, for I think she's a witch."

Margaret shuddered.

"Oh, don't! Whenever you talk about her, I feel I'm back in that awful orphanage. I'm sure the Matron we had there was a witch."

"Watch out, then," said Liza, "for they say they never die, but once they've 'ad you in their clutches, they come back!"

13. A Letter

Afterward Margaret could not remember much about the first night. At the dress rehearsal a lot had gone wrong, not mistakes by Margaret but by other people, such as lighting effects and actors forgetting their parts. Margaret herself nearly made a mistake, but Simon saved her. He carried her train in the cathedral and saw that she was going to start to move too soon, so he gave the train a smart tug to remind her.

A first night, Margaret learned, was in many ways the same if it was in a tent or in the much grander atmosphere of The Dolphin Theater. Everybody was nervous and overstrained. The theater felt as a garden feels before a thunderstorm. But once the audience had settled down and all the ladies' dresses had rustled into silence and the last gentleman had closed his opera hat and put it under his seat. Margaret felt a warmth between herself and the audience. Only a little at first, but by the time they reached the scene where she lost her temper, quite an outpouring. It felt wonderful.

By the time they reached the last act, Margaret was over the moon. Everything had gone well. The rest of the cast, as they passed her, had said graciously, "Well done, dear," and even Sir John had given her a pleased pat on the back. Now that the first night was almost over, Margaret felt in the mood to celebrate by doing something silly.

She was brought down to earth by her dresser, Ivy.

"Now stand still, child, do. This dress is hard enough to fasten with all these buttons down the back without your jumping and spinning around.

Margaret laughed.

"But I feel like jumping and spinning."

Ivy gave a look at Sarah.

"You talk to her, Mrs. Beamish."

Sarah laid aside the needlework she did in the theater.

"Stand still, Margaret," she said. "That dress is not easy to fasten, and Ivy has to be ready when she has put your train on to carry it down to the stage."

"No joke, that isn't," said Ivy, "for, of course, until you are on stage, it's not to touch the floor."

"Suppose," Margaret teased, "I won't stand still?"

"That's easy," said Sarah. "Liza goes on. With that crown and all, nobody would know the difference."

"But what about when we bow at the end?"

"Well, you wouldn't be there, would you?"

This brought Margaret down to earth with a bump. Like Queen Victoria, she almost said, "I will be good," but instead she murmured, "Sorry, I won't fidget again."

The play was a success but not a great success. Some of the critics were unkind to it, finding the actual writing heavy and old-fashioned. But about one thing all the critics agreed, and that was that Margaret was a real discovery.

"This little girl," one of the critics said, "plays with a

naturalness and charm which is a lesson to many actresses three times her age."

Another wrote, "When little Miss Thursday was on the stage, this play took on new life and meaning."

To Sarah's surprise Margaret took her success very calmly. The first-night excitement being over, she settled down into accepting—as she had when she had acted in *Little Lord Fauntleroy*—that, though she was proud of herself because she was Margaret Thursday, she was not proud of herself as an actress. That was something different altogether.

The day after the first night Sarah delivered Margaret to the schoolroom as usual. All the servants had been to the first night and had been very impressed by Margaret's performance. In one jump they had elevated her from "that child who does lessons with our Miss Katie" to "Miss Katie's little friend Margaret." When Sarah brought her to the private entrance to the theater the door was opened by Hilton, the butler. He smiled broadly at Margaret.

"We were all there last night, miss, and we thought you ever so good. Mrs. Melly said to tell you she's sending up a cake lunchtime that she's made special, and Annie"—Annie was the parlormaid—"she couldn't get over how you looked in your coronation dress."

"You tell her," said Margaret, "she wouldn't like it so much if she had to wear it. I have to be put in it, for I can't move properly when it's on."

Katie and Miss Grey had seen Margaret after the play the night before, but they were delighted to see her in the schoolroom.

"I had thought you would be tired, dear, and have a long lie in bed," said Miss Grey.

"I was afraid you wouldn't come," Katie agreed. "I am so glad you have, it's dull when you don't."

Sarah, when the girls weren't listening, said to Miss Grey, "I thought while you took Katie to her music this afternoon that you might put Margaret to have a lie-down with a book. She must be tired though she doesn't seem it."

That day the letter came. Margaret had given Lavinia the theater address, and knowing she was doing lessons with Katie, Bill Todd had sent Margaret's letter up with the family mail, being careful to draw Henry's attention to the crest on the flap of the envelope.

"See that," he said as he passed the letter over. "Our Margaret may have been found in a basket, but she knows some of the right people."

Lavinia's letter read just as if she were talking.

We are all so happy, it's as if those awful days never happened. Grandfather still has not found proof that we are his grandchildren, but he says he knows we are and that's all that matters. None of us care. I do not really want to be Lady Lavinia. Imagine how all those I worked with at Sedgecombe Place would laugh. My governess is very nice, and so is our tutor, and we spend glorious days riding around the estate. Now for my most important news. In the first week after Christmas Grandfather is bringing us all to London to see a pantomime and, of course, your play, so wait for a knock on your dressing-room door, it will be us. With much love, your affectionate friends,

Lavinia, Peter, Horatio

79

14. Christmas

Business was fairly good, though the theater was never packed. Then the Christmas plans were announced. Over Christmas there would be performances twice daily four times a week. After that, all day long people bought seats, for *The Little Queen* would, they thought, be just the play to which to take the children.

The theater would be closed on Christmas Day, and Sarah began worrying what she was to do for Margaret over Christmas. She could see that her stocking was filled, take her to church, and give her a Christmas dinner, but there was not much fun in that, just her and Mrs. Wallow. Then, the week before Christmas, Katie, her eyes shining, gave Margaret an invitation.

"Mama says I may ask you to stay here for Christmas. You could stay the two nights, Christmas Eve and Christmas Day. Oh, do say yes. It would be so gay if you could."

Of course Margaret could, and she was enchanted by the offer.

"Imagine, Sarah, all that at Christmas, and in the week after, Lavinia and the boys are coming. Aren't I lucky?"

Sarah was overjoyed at the way things had turned out.

Now she could spend Christmas with Lou, and they would go to a theatrical party on Christmas evening.

"Very lucky, dear, but you deserve it. A very good girl you've been."

Margaret had the best Christmas she had known. Where she had been brought up, the old ladies had tried to make a happy day for her and so had Hannah and the rector, but it had not been so easy when there was one small child with so many grown-ups.

"I never spent Christmas at that orphanage," Margaret told Katie, "but I believe all they had was one orange each."

"Poor things!" said Katie. "Do you think if ever you made a lot of money you would go and visit the orphanage?"

Margaret shivered as if a goose had walked over her grave.

"I don't know. I did hate it there so much, I wouldn't want even to visit."

On Christmas morning Miss Grey, true to her vicarage upbringing, took the girls to church, and by the time they got home, Mrs. Melly was dishing up the Christmas dinner. It was a gay, laughing meal, for several theater people came in for it, and even Lady Teaser seemed to enjoy it.

In the evening they had the Christmas tree. It was beautifully dressed, glittering with ornaments and blazing with candles; in fact, so many candles that Hilton and Henry stood by with mops and pails of water in case one set fire to the tree.

Everybody had presents. First of all the staff. Each woman received an apron except Mrs. Melly, who was above aprons and instead had a silk dress-length. Then they each had personal presents. Cuff links for the men with special initials, and trinkets for the women. Katie had her own presents for them all: fine handkerchiefs with the edges hand-rolled by herself.

When the general present-giving began, Margaret received so many presents that Miss Grey had to show her how to put the names of the givers on each one so she would know whom to thank. The one she liked best came from Ireland. It was a beautiful dress-length, homespun in soft colors, and was sent by Lavinia, Peter, and Horatio. There was a cold collation in the evening so the staff could enjoy their Christmas dinner. After the cold supper everybody who could, performed. Katie played the piano beautifully, Lady Teaser sang a ballad, Sir John recited, and some of the guests danced. The only people who could do nothing were Margaret and Miss Grey.

"You'll have to learn something by next year," said Sir John. "Can't have back-sliders."

Margaret smiled happily. Next year! Did Sir John think she would still be here? It was a splendid thought.

When she kissed Katie good night, she said, "You'll never, never know how much I've enjoyed today. I felt as if I were family. And I've still got Lavinia, Peter, and Horatio to look forward to."

A week later, just as they had promised, Lavinia, Peter, and Horatio and their grandfather knocked on Margaret's dressing-room door. They had been to the one-thirty performance because Grandfather thought the evening show would be too late for Horatio.

"Not that it made any difference," Peter said. "Horatio slept all the way through, anyway."

Horatio knew Margaret would understand.

"I was sick as sick on the boat to England. That's why I slept."

Margaret could not get over how well they all looked. When she had last seen them, bad food at the orphanage and the hard life of leggers had made the boys pasty-faced and hollow-eyed, and Lavinia had been worn out with worry while the boys were missing. Now they so shone with good health that it was a joy to look at them. All the same, although they looked so well, she had a feeling that Lavinia was worrying about something.

Lady Teaser, still hoping that Katie would make friends with Margaret's startlingly well-connected friends, had ordered a special tea to be served in the schoolroom. Mrs. Melly had been given carte blanche to serve what she thought fit, and she had let herself go. Lord Delaware laughed when he saw the table.

"You have indeed done us proud, Lady Teaser. We are simple folk in Ireland, and for tea we seldom have more than a plate of potato cakes and a soda loaf."

While Margaret was washing before tea, Lavinia crept into the bathroom after her.

"Could you ask Grandfather," she whispered, "if I could stay with you until the play starts? It's something I found out. Peter thinks, and I think, too, that you ought to know."

Margaret stared at Lavinia, while it felt as if ice were slipping down her back.

"You've seen Mr. Fortescue? He's found out where I am?"

Lavinia shook her head.

"Worse, far worse. Let's plan so I can see you in your dressing room before you have to go onstage again."

15. Precautions

Margaret found it difficult to behave as if nothing had happened. Something worse than Mr. Fortescue having found her! What could be worse than that? Imagine if he said she was engaged to act for him and made her go back to act in his fit-up company! Luckily, Horatio had so much to say about being seasick, and Katie wanted to know so much about Ireland, it was hard for Margaret to get in a word, anyway.

In a pause Margaret did remember to ask Lord Delaware if Lavinia could sit with her in her dressing room until the curtain went up.

Lord Delaware shook his head.

"I'm sorry, my child, but that would mean Lavinia would be walking herself home, and I would not be allowing that."

Miss Grey intervened.

"I'm sure Sarah will walk with Lavinia to the hotel. It won't take her more than a few minutes."

It was not long afterward that the tea party broke up, though to Lavinia it felt like hours, but at last the good-byes were said, and Lavinia and Margaret were alone. Then Margaret said, her chin up to take what was coming. "Well?"

Lavinia drew a chair up to the dressing table. She spoke very quietly so no one could overhear what she said. "When we got to the theater, Grandfather took the boys to the place where they could leave their coats. I waited for them by where they sell the tickets. It was then that I saw her. She looked simply awful, almost as if she were mad. She had a little boy with her, and she was reading one of those lists that says who was acting in the play. I kept out of sight behind people, but I got quite close to her and saw her point to a name. Then she said to the little boy, 'Read it, read it.' The little boy did not want to, he was scared and halfcrying but at last he said, 'Margaret Thursday. Like I told you, it says Margaret Thursday.' The woman gave a sort of growl, and then she said in a sort of mutter, 'I'll get her. You wait and see, I'll get her.' Then she pushed her way through the people coming in and, dragging the little boy behind her, vanished in the crowd. Oh, Margaret, I wouldn't have told you, but it was Matron, Matron from the orphanage."

Although she had rouge on her cheeks, Margaret had turned quite pale.

"Matron! Oh, Lavinia!"

Lavinia got up and put her arms around her.

"I did not tell you to scare you but just to warn you to be careful. Do not ever go about alone."

"I never do. Anyway, what would Matron want me for?"

"You always said she hated you. Perhaps she wants to punish you for running away. I wonder if she is still at the orphanage."

"Sure to be. But I've had all her worst punishments. I

suppose I could have them all again. If she could catch me, that is."

"Do not be silly," said Lavinia. "Never give her a chance to get near you. Peter said, when I told him that, she sounded much madder than when we were in the orphanage."

"I think I'll tell Sarah," said Margaret. "She's a very sensible person and so is her sister Lou. I would feel safer if they knew. You see, when you go back to Ireland, I'll be alone."

Lavinia thought telling Lou a good idea.

"And I'd tell Katie's governess. I like her. I'm sure she'll know exactly what to do."

The door opened and Liza's cheeky face looked in.

"Thought I'd warn you, but they're soon calling the overture, and Ivy's waiting to put on your dress."

Lavinia got up to join Sarah, who was waiting in the passage. As she kissed Margaret good-bye she whispered, "Tell Liza. I'm sure she'll help."

Mrs. Wallow always left their supper in the oven. That night, while they were eating, Margaret told Sarah what Lavinia had said. To her surprise, Sarah took the news calmly.

"If you had said you'd seen the woman, knowing what a one you are for storytelling, I wouldn't have believed you, but Lavinia's different. A quiet young lady she is, not given to fancifying. But now we know that there's nothing to worry about, we just got to be careful, that's all. But to be on the safe side I'll have a word with Mr. Todd. He never does let anyone, who has not the right, in at the stage door, but 'e may well be extra careful."

Because it was Christmastime, there were no lessons, so Margaret was able to spend her mornings with Lavinia, Peter, and Horatio. In the afternoons when she didn't have a performance, she saw two matinees with them, the pantomime *The Sleeping Beauty and the Beast* with the great comedian Dan Leno at Drury Lane Theatre Royal, and the musical comedy *Floradora* at The Lyric. She loved both and came out of the theaters wondering if she should not learn to sing and dance. Sarah quietly killed that idea.

"You can be thankful for what you can do, dear. For a musical you want to start real young. Lou was working when she was three."

Miss Grey volunteered to take the children sight-seeing in the mornings, for which Lord Delaware was very grateful.

"Tis wonderfully pleased I am. I find that a little walking around London is nearly the death of me. There are all too many people around trampling the streets."

Lady Teaser was also enthusiastic that Katie should join the sight-seeing expeditions.

"It will be pleasant for Katie, such nice children. I want them to be friends."

On those sight-seeing trips no one was better guarded than Margaret. Peter walked on one side of her and Lavinia on the other, and behind came Miss Grey with Horatio and Katie.

"Do not worry at all," Miss Grey told Margaret. "The moment I heard of this horrid woman I invested in a police whistle. Look."

Then she opened her jacket to show a police whistle at the ready, as it were, pinned to the lining.

Though Margaret did not know it, everybody did not take Margaret's danger lightly.

"I don't like it," said Lou when Sarah told her the story. "I thought young Margaret was pitching a tale when she told us about that Matron, but maybe she was not. There's a lot of evil people in the world and you can't be too careful. You'd better see that her window is bolted of a night time."

Sarah usually exchanged a few words with Bill Todd during the show but, to tell him about Margaret's troubles, she took a special expedition to his little room during the last act, when Margaret never left the stage.

"Could I have a quiet word with you, Mr. Todd?"

Bill had a bottle of port. He held it out.

"Would you fancy a drop, Mrs. Beamish?"

Sarah said she would, and Bill opened his door and sat on his box and gave Sarah the chair.

Sarah settled down and supped her port.

"It may be true or it could be a mare's nest as the saying goes." Then she told him the story just as Lavinia had told it to Margaret. "I thought I'd like you to know just in case, like."

Bill poured himself out some more port.

"You done right in telling me; if that little Lady Lavinia says that it is what she saw and heard, then it's Bible truth. She wouldn't make nothing up, that she wouldn't. And you done right to tell me 'cause I'll be extra careful on my door. There's many bad people around Mrs. Beamish. You can't be too careful."

Liza was another who took Margaret's danger seriously.

"You want to watch it. You don't know who you is. Might be heir to a fortune you might. Anyways, the world is full of shockers, and that Matron sounds like one. You can't be too careful. Now, you take my advice, never be ashamed to scream. Better scream than have your throat cut, is my motto."

Margaret tried not to sound scared.

"Trust me," she promised, "I'll scream."

16. A Scare

Like all other actor-managers, Sir John thought a long
way ahead. He decided that with any luck *The Little Queen*
would run until after Easter, but he wanted something to
take its place. Something, he thought wistfully, like *Little
Lord Fauntleroy*, in which he could build on Margaret's
success as The Little Queen. But no play was sent to him
to read that had a child's part in it, and he began to feel
he would have to give up his idea of using Margaret.

Then Tommy Smith made a suggestion.

"Why not put on *The Tempest*? You will be a magnifi-
cent Prospero. There is enormous scope for the lavish
production your public expect of you, and Margaret can
play Ariel."

"By Jove, Tommy, I think you're right. I have always
wanted to play Prospero, and we really can let our-
selves go on the decorations, that island just asks for
it." Then he looked thoughtful. "But I don't believe I
see Margaret as Ariel. She is full of good qualities, but
I don't see anything magical about her. Her great gift
is her reality. She puts both feet solidly on the stage
and becomes a real person and makes the cast believe
in themselves. Several of them have mentioned it. But

Ariel is a creature of the elements—all spirit. Could Margaret play the part?"

Tommy could see in his mind's eye Katie. Little slim Katie as she had looked when she played Puck. Never human, never of this earth.

"The trouble is," he said, "it's difficult to see Margaret in the role because we see someone else who was born to play the part."

Sir John made a face.

"It's no good thinking of it, Tommy. Her ladyship has made up her mind, and I am not bringing the subject up again. But I'll tell Miss Grey to put the girls on to study *The Tempest*, and that will mean by the time I am ready to hear Margaret read the part, she will have some idea of what it is all about."

Though it was not talked about, Miss Grey was nervous when she took the children out. She had, of course, never seen the orphanage Matron and only had Lavinia's word for it that she was in London, but she could see that Margaret believed she was around, from the way she kept close to her side and kept glancing behind her. Because it was still the Christmas holiday, Miss Grey had to take the girls out whenever it was fine, but she much preferred it when they amused themselves in the schoolroom.

What frightened her most was when they went to afternoon performances in a bus. They always drove both ways, but, when leaving a theater, it was only too easy to get separated for a moment by the crowds.

Katie had not been told anything about Livinia thinking that she had seen the Matron. Much better not to worry her, Miss Grey had decided. It is not as though she would be any help; if the Matron does make an attempt to kidnap Margaret, there are enough of them to see that she does not succeed. Then she comforted herself by feeling for her police whistle.

It was the police whistle that put Katie on to the fact that something odd was happening. Katie was nobody's fool, and very soon she had seen that something was pinned under Miss Grey's jacket. She was helped by the fact that every few minutes Miss Grey's hand shot up to be sure it was still there. Katie would probably never have known it was a police whistle if, just as Miss Grey was giving it a furtive feel, Henry had not come in with elevenses on a silver tray. Miss Grey put her hand down so suddenly that the whistle caught on her little finger, and for a second it was exposed to Katie's view.

Katie said nothing but accepted the glass of milk and biscuits Henry handed her. But after he had gone, she put her mind to the problem. She had never seen a police whistle, but she knew the police carried them. She had both seen and owned whistles, especially the sort that sang like songbirds, particularly cuckoos. But what would Miss Grey be doing with a whistle?

That afternoon there was a matinee. It was a shocking day, raining cats and dogs and with a wind full of sleet. Lady Teaser was out playing cards and was not expected back until about six, so Miss Grey—sorry for Katie cooped up in the house—let her go down and sit with Margaret while she got dressed for the play.

Katie stayed on for a short while, after Margaret had gone to the stage, to talk to Liza. She did not know Liza well but she enjoyed talking to her, and today she had something to find out.

"Liza, what does a police whistle look like?"

Liza was caught off-balance, for she had been talking about something quite different.

"A police whistle? Why?"

Katie had to giggle.

"Because I think Miss Grey is wearing one."

Katie expected Liza to roar with laughter, for the very idea was funny, but instead she hesitated. She knew Katie had not been told what was feared; how was she to explain a police whistle? Then she had an idea.

"Lots of ladies wear them," she said, "same as lots wouldn't get into bed without they sees if there's a burglar under it. Single ladies like Miss Grey, they 'as to be careful on account they have no 'usband to look after them."

"Well, Miss Grey has only just taken to wearing one, and I think it's odd."

Liza felt on firm ground.

"I don't. There's terrible types about the streets these days. And you don't hurry up them stairs, she'll be blowing her whistle for you."

When the girls' lessons began again, Miss Grey started them studying *The Tempest*.

"Why *The Tempest*?" Katie asked. "You said we'd do *As You Like It* this term."

"Nothing is decided," Miss Grey explained, "but when *The Little Queen* comes off, there is just a chance that your father might produce *The Tempest*. He wishes to play Prospero."

Margaret's heart sank. Shakespeare! What in her innermost heart she called "that awful Shakespeare." However, she did not say anything, for it would sound—which indeed it was—a groan, because she would be out of work.

"Is there a child in it?" she asked without much hope.

"It depends on how Papa plays it," Katie explained. "There is Ariel. Papa has said it should be played by a child, but I think he thinks it should be a boy."

"I like being a boy," said Margaret. "I loved being Little Lord Fauntleroy."

Miss Grey realized that Margaret had never even read the play and decided nothing would be gained by discussing her chances.

"Ariel is a spirit, neither child nor adult, neither boy nor girl."

"And you would have to sing," said Katie, and crooned, "Full fathom five thy father lies."

Miss Grey stopped her.

"No singing now, Katie. We're going to do sums."

That evening, walking home with Sarah, Margaret told her what Miss Grey had said about *The Tempest*. Sarah, too, had heard gossip.

"I think it's only talk at present, dear, and nothing may come of it, but they do say Sir John hasn't a new play he wants to do, and when he finds what he wants, he'd like to find one with a part for you, seeing as he found you in the first place. You were very nicely wrote about in the papers. So he discovered you, as it were."

Up went Margaret's chin.

"If anybody found me, it was Mr. and Mrs. Fortescue. But, really, nobody did. I found myself, and it was you who put me in The Dolphin Theater." Margaret was silent for a few steps, then she went on. "If Sir John doesn't find a play with a part for me, how do I look for work in another theater?"

Sarah really did not know, for she, herself, between theater engagements had always worked in some theater wardrobe. But she had talked over the problem with Lou.

"There are sorts of schools where they teach you acting and dancing and that and find you work. We'll have to inquire of Mr. Smith about them. It's no good asking me about this Shakespeare. I never had nothing to do with him."

They had reached Miss de Lang's auntie's house. Sarah stepped forward to put her key in the front door, but before she got it out of her reticule, Mrs. Wallow flung the door open.

"Oh, there you are! I'm ever so glad to see you. There's something funny going on."

Sarah managed to keep a tremble out of her voice.

"What sort of funny?"

"It was the people next door told me. They said when I was out shopping, an old woman was 'anging around asking questions about Margaret. They thought we ought to know, for they said she looked like a witch."

17. Margaret's Gone

Sarah had a fearful night, jumping upright every time she heard a creak. She had no idea what Margaret's Matron would look like, but she knew what she supposed a witch would look like, and her teeth chattered. Twice she nearly screamed because she thought she heard steps creeping up the stairs.

Margaret appeared to show no signs of being frightened but ate her supper as heartily as usual. The truth was that Margaret, though scared, could not imagine Matron hanging around out-of-doors on a winter's night. She had liked her comfort, had Matron. It was nasty if she had found out where she lived. Tomorrow they must take precautions, but now that they were safely locked in, she tried not to think about her and in the middle of trying she had fallen asleep.

The next morning it was awkward explaining to Mrs. Wallow what had happened, for Sarah was afraid that Mrs. Wallow might not like renting her rooms to people who had a witch inquiring after them. However, Mrs. Wallow in daylight seemed quite calm.

"Terrible what goes on in orphanages," she said, "but I'll have a word with my hubby. As you know, he's night watchman to a place not far from here. He'll come to the entrance to the square and meet you."

As things turned out, there was no need for anyone to meet Margaret. The moment she had delivered her for her lessons, Sarah hurried around to the stage door to pour out her troubles to Bill Todd. He listened in silence until she had finished, then he said, "You did right to tell me, Sarah"—he had never called her Sarah before—"but this is too much responsibility for us. I'll just get the fireman to come around from the front to look after the door, and then we'll go up and you'll tell Mr. Smith what you've told me. He'll know what should be done."

"Oh, thank you, Bill," said Sarah, not noticing that she had used his Christian name.

Of course Tommy Smith had to be told the whole story, starting at the beginning when Lavinia had seen Matron. When Sarah had told all she knew, he thought for a bit and then said, "You must know a trusty growler driver, don't you, Bill?"

"That I do," Bill agreed, "a relative of my sister's 'usband he is."

"Do you know how to get hold of him?"

Bill nodded.

"Has his dinner at The Pig and Whistle. I could leave a message there for him."

"Good," said Mr. Smith. "Who's on the door now?"

"I got the fireman."

"Right. Well, tell him to stay on there and you pop along to The Pig and Whistle and tell your friend to call each night at curtain fall to pick up a young lady and her . . ." He hesitated, not knowing how to describe Sarah.

"Friend," Sarah suggested.

"Friend," Mr. Smith agreed, "and tell him when he comes to the stage door tonight, he is to ask Mrs. Beamish for her house key, unlock the door, and see Margaret and Mrs. Beamish safely inside before he leaves!"

On the stairs on the way back to the stage door Sarah stopped.

"There! I never asked him about paying. I'll manage, of course, but will it cost a lot?"

Bill smiled.

"You didn't order the growler. Mr. Smith did, so he'll pay, and what's more, he'll find the money out of the little cash box what he keeps, and Sir John won't be a penny the wiser."

"You don't think he'll tell Sir John?"

Bill dismissed that idea.

" 'Course he won't. If Sir John knew of Margaret's little worry, he'd call out the whole of the police force and a private detective and I don't know what else. And we mustn't forget Lady Lavinia is only a child and she may have imagined what she thinks she saw. Anyway, best not trouble Sir John."

Liza had stuck to her promise, and each day she wandered around Covent Garden until she found Simon and could give him Katie's and Margaret's gift of food.

"I'm glad to 'ave it to give," she told Margaret. "Now it's turned so cold, the poor little thing is blue, for 'e hasn't much on."

"I wonder he doesn't stay in the house until it's time to go to the theater."

There was scorn in Liza's voice.

"Chance is a good thing. I reckon that Ma Mud sends 'im and any of the others who is not workin' out in the streets to beg. She won't want 'im 'angin' around indoors, an' I don't suppose there is any fire."

The cold weather turned to fog, and in those days, London fogs were famous. They were called pea-soupers because they were thick as pea soup and the whole air was yellow. Somehow all the cast got to the theater, and somehow Horace, the growler driver, got Margaret and Sarah home each evening.

"I thank God each night in my prayers," Sarah told Margaret, "for Mr. Horace. Imagine, in this fog, getting you safely home!"

The cast might somehow get to the theater, but the weather was too much for many of the audience. To stumble through banks of frozen snow piled on the pavements was one thing, but to cross roads when you had no chance to see what was coming was another. So many stayed away.

"We can't go on like this," Sir John said, studying the sheets of paper showing how much money had been taken at the box office, "or I'll be broke."

Tommy knew how much money Sir John had in the bank and was now worried. All the same, no manager could afford to run his theater at a loss. And he had to bear in mind that the previous play had lost money in its last weeks.

"Thought any more about *The Tempest*? The scenery and all, that will set us back a bit, but there are plenty of first-class actors to be had cheap, and with Shakespeare there are no royalties to eat up the profits."

"I would have liked to cash in on Margaret's success, but I don't see her as Ariel."

Tommy had never cared for *The Tempest*, so he had never imagined anyone playing Ariel.

"They all say you ought to play Prospero, so I don't suppose Margaret will make all that difference. I suggest you put her under contract and we can fix work for her with other managements until we find a new part for her. The Pinkertons are going on the road, slap-up tour, and George Pinkerton has been asking what plans you have for Margaret. He wants to add *Romeo and Juliet* to his repertory. He's a good coach is old Pinkerton, a tour with him would do Margaret good."

At that moment there were the sounds of running feet in the passage, and Katie, white and trembling, came into the room. She flung herself onto her father.

"Papa! Papa! Margaret's gone, that Matron has got her!"

18. The Search Begins

That morning Sarah and Margaret had started off to work early, for no one could hurry in the fog, and Miss Grey liked lessons to begin punctually. Mrs. Wallow had come to the door to see them off.

"Oh, it's worse than ever," she said in dismay when she saw the fog. "What we need is a good gale to blow it away. I wish you needn't go out in it."

"Better we go now than later," said Sarah. "It seems to get thicker as the day goes on."

Margaret put an arm around Sarah.

"Come on. I'll look after you, but I won't let you go and see Lou. You'll go and sit with Mrs. Melly. You know she likes it when you do."

Fumbling, Margaret and Sarah moved toward the gate when they heard a sound. They both stood still straining their ears.

"It can't be," said Mrs. Wallow.

"If it is, it's a miracle," murmured Sarah.

Margaret moved toward the gate.

"Hi!" she called. "Hi! Are you a cab?"

Out of the murkiness came a fruity voice.

"I am. Where was you wanting to go?"

Margaret told him.

"Oh, please take us."

The cabby climbed down from his box.

"All right then, in you go."

He opened the cab door, shoved Margaret inside, and slammed the door.

"I am going too," Sarah called out.

The cabman gave her a push, which sent her sprawling back across the pavement, then he climbed up to his seat, and disregarding the row going on in his cab, he drove off.

Margaret did her best to scream, but something was shoved into her mouth. She fought like a savage to open the cab door, but she could not release her hands from an iron grip.

Then a voice spoke—a voice she had never forgotten.

"No good fighting, Margaret Thursday. I still have my strength, but I've you to thank for losing me everything else, so now you're going to pay for it."

After they were well clear of the square, the driver pulled up his cab and opened the cab door. Then he tied Margaret up. He put strong rope around her legs and wrists, and the small gag was taken from her mouth and a larger, evil-tasting one shoved in its place and then securely bandaged into position.

"Throw her on the floor," said the voice Margaret now knew as being Matron's. "She won't be seen there, and I can keep my feet on her and give her a kick if she moves."

Back at the theater, anxious consultations were taking place. The police were told, and came around at once to learn what they could from Sarah, but Sarah had not always listened to what she called Margaret's tales.

"I don't know where the orphanage is where Margaret was, though she told me often enough. Do you remember, Miss Katie? She must have told you."

"She did," Katie agreed, "but I am afraid it won't help. It was called St. Luke's and was a home for one hundred boys and girls of Christian background."

"She never mentioned a town, miss?" the constable asked.

Katie tried to remember.

"I don't think she knew a place. The orphans were marched to school, so I suppose there was a village, but she never said what it was called."

"What she did talk of was where Lord and Lady Corkberry lived," Sarah remembered. "She had some tale about Miss Lavinia—Lord Delaware's granddaughter, that is—being a scullery maid there, but I always thought it was just one of Margaret's tales."

"It wasn't," said Katie. "It was true. Lavinia told me herself, and she told me about the wicked Matron and—"

The constable stopped her.

"It's that Matron we are anxious to interview. If we knew where that orphanage is, we might find it's there that she has taken the little girl."

"We know it's by a canal," Katie said. "You see, when Margaret and the boys escaped from the orphanage, it was at night, and so they followed the canal."

"Come to that," said Sarah, "they lived later on a canal boat. They used to lead the horse, Margaret said."

Tommy Smith could see that the constable was getting confused.

"I think you will get the information you want from Lord and Lady Corkberry. There seems no doubt that Lord Delaware's granddaughter did work for them, so they would know the address of the orphanage for she probably came from there."

"Meanwhile," said the constable, "we are carrying out a wide search in London. The man we want is the cab-driver who drove the child away." He turned to Sarah. "You're sure you don't remember anything about him? How did he speak?"

This was something Sarah could answer with certainty.

"He was a Cockney, rough-speaking he was."

"But you never got a look at him?"

Sarah was scornful.

"In this fog! Anyway, when I moved to get into the cab, he gave me a push, which sent me sprawling, and by the time I was up, the cab was gone. Me and Mrs. Wallow listened, but we couldn't hear a sound. She wanted me to come back into the house and have a drop of brandy, but I said no, we must start a search right away, so I came here just as fast as I could."

"We have sent a constable to interview Mrs. Wallow," the policeman told Tommy Smith. Then he closed his book. "There's no more I can do here for the present. You'll be hearing, sir, the moment we know anything."

Margaret, lying on the cab floor, was not frightened but blazingly angry. How dare Matron put her dirty boots on her, Margaret Thursday! How dare she kidnap her! She was not in the orphanage now. She was an actress earning her own living. Then, as the cab turned into a busy street, Margaret stopped thinking how angry she was and attended to the traffic. If she listened, could she tell where she was? At first the sounds were confusing: the clop of horses' feet mixed with shouts from drivers who could not see clearly and needed a passageway through the fog. But presently she heard new sounds: men shouting, the banging of boxes, the rumble of heavy carts. For a few moments she could not remember why the sounds were familiar, then it came back to her. They were somewhere near where Lou lived. They were in Covent Garden.

If only I could turn over and get a look outside, she thought. *even in the fog I'd get an idea which road I was in. Besides, if I could turn over, I could bite Matron's leg. . . .*

That was the moment when, in answer to a shouted "whoa" from the driver, the horse stopped.

19. A Telegram for Liza

Liza seldom went to school. Her mother always had an excuse ready: one of the babies was ill and she had to keep Liza at home to help out, or Liza had been having private lessons. Any lie would do that could pacify the attendance man sent to find where she was. On the day Margaret was missing, Liza's mother had a job, so Liza was at home cooking the children's dinner, for all eight had been kept at home while the fog lasted. When there was a knock on the door, Liza sent one of the younger children to answer it.

"Tell 'im we've 'ad measles. I'll hide in the other room."

Liza ran into the bedroom and pressed her ear to the door to hear a boy's voice say, "Telegram for Miss Wigan."

A telegram could come from only one place, and that was The Dolphin. Liza dashed back into the kitchen and snatched the telegram from the boy and tore it open. It said, "Come at once to theater you will be playing tonight. Smith."

Liza sent the eldest boy off to find his mother to tell her what had happened. Then, shutting all the other children in the kitchen, she went into the bedroom to change into her theater-going clothes.

Here's a turn-up, she thought. What can have happened to Margaret? Right as a trivet she was last night. She put on the clean underclothes her mother always kept ready for an emergency. Don't want that la-di-da Ivy turning up her nose, she thought.

The fog was lifting slightly, so Liza ran all the way to the theater and burst through the stage door panting for breath.

"Oh, Mr. Todd, what's wrong with Margaret?"

Instructions had been given that no one was to mention that Margaret was missing. The story put out was that she had a chill. Even if there had been no story put out, Bill Todd was not having any jumped-up understudy forgetting her place.

"Good morning, Miss Wigan. Mr. Gay is waiting for you on the stage. I believe Miss Thursday is confined to the house with a chill."

Liza was not that easily snubbed.

"You don't believe anythin' of the sort, but I've got to go now. I will be back to hear the truth later."

Edward Gay, the stage manager, was waiting for Liza. He knew her well because he supervised her understudy rehearsals.

"Morning, Liza. This is just a run-through for lines and, in your case, aitches. Don't you dare drop an aitch tonight or Sir John will have me hanged, drawn, and quartered."

Liza grinned at him.

"Don't fret, I can talk like a lady when I want, and you know it." Then she lowered her voice. "What's really the matter with Margaret? And I don't want to hear that she's got a chill. I've heard that one."

"That's what they've told me, and I've no reason to think it isn't true. Anyone could catch a chill in this weather."

Liza temporarily gave in.

"All right. Are we starting at the beginning?"

"Straight through, then later this afternoon you are to run through your scenes with Sir John."

Liza was right when she said she could talk properly when she had to. It was overrefined English. She was nowhere near as good an actress as Margaret, but once those who listened to her overcareful English were used to her, she had a perky charm.

The rehearsal over, Liza had hoped to find someone who would give her news of Margaret, but she was immediately sent to the wardrobe to have any alterations required made on the clothes.

It was while she was in the wardrobe that she noticed that her inside was rumbling, and she remembered it was dinnertime and she had no money to buy anything to eat. She could, she supposed, ask for a sub on her salary, but she did not want to do that. It was her pride to take home every Friday her two pounds intact. It was a pity that Mrs. Beamish was not around. She would have found her something to eat, but she would, of course, be at home looking after Margaret—or would she?

"There, that will be all," said the wardrobe mistress. "If the coronation dress doesn't fit, it can do the other thing, for none of us dares touch it."

Out in the passage Liza stood undetermined. Her inside was rumbling more than ever. She thought longingly of that stew she had been cooking, mainly vegetables mostly picked up by the children in the market, but there was a few pennyworth of scrag ends of meat. Liza could almost smell it, and it made her stomach turn over worse than ever.

There was the sound of clumping feet coming down the staircase, and in a few seconds Miss Grey came into sight. No instructions had been given to her or to Katie that they were to keep the fact that Margaret had been kidnapped to themselves, so, knowing that Liza had been told that Margaret was threatened, she burst out at once, "Oh, Liza, dear, isn't it dreadful? The police are getting in touch with that Lord and Lady Corkberry where Lavinia worked before her grandfather found her. They feel they will know where the orphanage is."

Liza was for once startled into silence. Then she asked, "How was she got at? Do they know it was that Matron?"

Miss Grey felt in some way that she had blundered.

"Oh, dear, you didn't know? I suppose I shouldn't have told you." Then a new thought struck her. "So inconsiderate of me thinking only of Margaret, for I suppose you are going to act in her place tonight."

Liza felt the need to hold on to someone, for the floor seemed to be going around. She clutched at Miss Grey, who, after a glance at her, led her to the stairs and sat her down.

"I suppose you have been rehearsing all the morning and have had no dinner. Ours is just coming up and you can have it with Katie and me. I shall be glad for someone to distract Katie, for she is in a terrible state of anxiety. Now just wait there a moment and I will call Henry to help you up the stairs. Poor child, what a day for you, with that long part to act and the worry over Margaret."

A little more life seemed to creep into Liza. She raised her head and looked Miss Grey firmly in the eye.

"I'm not worried about Margaret. She's not one to scare easy. I bet she'll give that Matron as good as she gets. You'll see."

20.　The Prisoner

Though Margaret had been busy trying to hear in which direction they were going, she had also made a plan for her arrival. *It's a busy part of London,* she thought. *She may think she'll take me in without anybody seeing, but if I can't shout, I can wriggle.*

It was a very rough, horribly dirty lane in which the cab stopped. Because the fog was at last lifting, the women were gathered outside gossiping about how bad the fog had been.

Although there were frequent street brawls when they knocked each other around, as a rule the women were friendly, for they shared two things in common: grinding poverty and a detestation of the police. About this last they ganged together. They might know a lot the police would like to hear, but they never said a word that might incriminate their neighbors. So when a cab drew up outside number four and the driver carried a struggling child, tied around the legs with rope, up the steps, and into the house, they all scattered. Only when the door was shut, and Margaret and Matron were inside, and the cab had driven away did they draw together again to mutter, "Poor kiddie." "That's another for 'er to starve." "It's a shame." "Somebody did ought to report 'er."

When the driver threw Margaret onto the floor, she knocked her head so badly that for a few seconds she was unconscious. When she regained her senses, Matron was muttering at her.

"I suppose you think you are somebody, acting a big part at The Dolphin Theater, but you'll learn different here. What I need in this house is a skivvy, to clean the place and wait on me. If you don't do exactly what I say, you'll be punished, and you know what my punishments are like. Now, I am going to untie your legs and wrists so you can make a start on the stairs, the dirt's that thick there, it might be a carpet."

While the ropes were being untied Margaret tried to think what it would be best to do. It was certain if she did not do what she was told she would be beaten. It was no good thinking of escape, for she had heard Matron lock the door after the cab had left. On the other hand, not for one single second was Matron to get away with the idea that she was giving in. She knew a skivvy was a very common way of describing a general maid. The poor little orphans that Matron had kept on after leaving age to work in the orphanage, they were skivvies, and what a life they had led! She, Margaret Thursday, would be nobody's skivvy, let Matron do what she liked with her.

Because Margaret did so love having lace on her petticoats, for Christmas Sarah had made lace for all her underclothes, something that pleased Margaret every morning when she put them on. That day she was wearing the warmest of what had been Katie's frocks: a darkish blue wool with a velvet band at the neck and a frill at the bottom of the skirt. Now, lying on what smelled like a very dirty floor and feeling Matron's hands fumbling with the ropes around her ankles and wrists, she was lifted out of her personal misery by pride. Wait until Matron saw how she was dressed. That would surprise her. She would pretend she was the Little Queen in the play. That would keep her chin up even if Matron dragged her all the way back to the orphanage.

The last knot was untied and the dirty gag taken out of Margaret's mouth. With an effort, for she was stiff from being tied up, she sat up, and all she wanted to say boiled up in her; then she saw that Matron and the boiling stopped.

Matron, as she had known her, had been a cruel-faced woman, rather plump because she fed herself well, and very well dressed for her position. The woman Margaret was now looking at was scraggy, with gray hair hanging in rats' tails around her shoulders. She wore a dirty, torn, woolen dress, and over it a large black shawl. Margaret would not have recognized her except for her snappy, beady eyes and her terribly cruel mouth. It was those eyes that kept her silent. She's mad, she thought. Whatever has happened to her, she's mad.

Back in the village where Margaret had been brought up there had been a mad woman. If left alone, she did no great harm, though her mutterings scared people. Margaret's guardian, the rector, made a point of visiting the mad woman regularly. "I don't do any good," he would say, "but I like her to feel she has a friend." Margaret had no wish that Matron should be looked upon as a friend but, if she was mad, she must not be made madder. She must be treated with cunning. Matron pointed to a door.

"You'll find a tap in there and a dishrag and basin, then get on your knees and scrub those stairs."

Margaret, with immense grandeur, her chin high in the air, went to do as she was told. *It's not me doing this,* she thought, comforting herself. *It's Anastasia.*

Poor Margaret needed all her imagination to believe that she was Anastasia. The house was appallingly squalid; just to touch the dish cloth when she found it made her think she was going to be sick. There was no hot water and nothing on which to heat a kettle, so she filled the basin with cold water from a dripping tap. She had no chance to explore, for before she had filled the basin, Matron was shouting, "Hurry up, Margaret Thursday, or you'll get a beating you won't forget."

For the rest of her life Margaret remembered cleaning those stairs. When she was filling the basin, she had noticed a broken knife on the floor. She had picked it up and hidden it under the dish cloth, thinking a weapon would come in handy. But its first use was to scrape the stairs, which had dirt so thick on them, it was, as Matron had described, like a carpet.

Before the stairs were half done, Matron was screaming at Margaret to hurry.

"I've got to go out to the shops and I can't leave you loose, so get on with it now."

Margaret decided that if Matron could live with stairs in that state, she wouldn't notice if the last part was only wiped over, so in a few minutes she got thankfully up off her knees. Her pretty frock was creased and dirty where she had knelt on it. *But I don't care,* she thought. *The first thing I shall do when I escape is to burn every scrap of clothing I have worn in this terrible house.*

Matron had always been a strong woman, but now her madness seemed to give her extra strength. Though Margaret fought every inch of the way, she dragged her into the room where she had been sent to get water and, with the rope that the cabman had tied around her, she fastened her securely to an old mangle.

"Pull that over if you want to," she said. "It will fall on you, so if you're hurt, you've only yourself to blame."

Margaret could see that Matron was not in her right mind, but she still could not imagine why she was in such a fury with her.

"I'm not a fool," she said. "I can see it would do no good to pull your mangle over—but why me? What have I done to you?"

A curious noise came out of Matron, more like the screech of a big bird than a human cry.

"What have you done? Who told lies and put that Lady Corkberry on to having me dismissed without money or a character? Who put the orphans on to throwing vegetables and that at me as I drove away? Who put the police on to me pretending to be drowned in the canal?"

Margaret was astonished.

"I didn't know you weren't Matron at the orphanage anymore. Thank goodness you aren't, for you were mean and cruel, but I didn't know."

Matron slapped Margaret's face.

"Be quiet, you. There'll be more work for you to do when I get back."

Margaret heard the front door key turn in its lock. She was horribly uncomfortable, for at the slightest movement her wrists ached from the rope that tied them. There was nothing for it, she decided, but to be perfectly

116

still. It was then that she heard a sound, a sort of scuffling and rustling. Margaret stiffened, and for a second her courage deserted her. Then she managed to raise her chin a little.

"All right," she called out. "I can hear you." She managed to keep the tremble out of her voice. "I am Margaret Thursday and I'm never afraid of anything—not even rats."

21. The Search Goes On

Of course the fact that Margaret had been kidnapped could not be kept secret. Mrs. Wallow told the neighbors, and the neighbors told their neighbors. In the kitchen of the private part of The Dolphin, the news soon reached the staff, and Annie slipped out to tell her boyfriend, and Hilton told the innkeeper when he had his midday glass of port. But, though she did not realize that she had done it, the one who really spread the news was Sarah.

The moment the fog lifted, Sarah went as fast as her legs would carry her to Lou in the wardrobe of the London Hippodrome. Lou turned quite gray when she heard the news, for she was more aware than most of the wicked things that went on in London's back streets. She looked so pale that Sarah thought she was going to faint, and called out for help. At once all the wardrobe staff gathered around with every imaginable remedy for faints and shock and they, of course, heard what had happened and, once Lou was better, could not wait to slip out into the street to spread the news.

Bill Todd had been told that Margaret was missing and that it was to be kept a secret for the present. "That for a tale," he had said to himself. "Someone will talk and then we'll have all the newspapers here." To prepare for the invasion he fastened a chain on the stage door. This meant he could see if anybody who belonged wanted to come in, but he could also keep out those who had no right of entry. When the press did arrive, he was thankful for his chain. Describing the scene later, he said it was like an election night. "Seemed as if there were hundreds all shouting outside my stage door." Of course, the press paid no attention to chains. There were other ways into the theater and they found them all, and soon Tommy Smith's office was crowded with men clamoring for information.

Because, in Tommy's opinion, honesty was the best policy, he told the newspaper men in truth. How Margaret had been kidnapped in a growler. How it was believed she had been taken to an orphanage where she had once lived. How she had begun her life in a basket with three of everything though all of the very best quality. How she had called herself Thursday because that was the day when she was found.

It was a wonderful story, and the newspaper men were delighted and rushed off to get their versions of it into the midday papers. Some of them lingered, hoping to get a statement from Sir John, but Tommy refused.

"He is upset enough as it is," he said, "and I have told you the truth as I know it. We must now leave matters to the police."

There were others who did not agree with Tommy Smith, and Lou was one of them. In spite of her great size, she got around and had often said, "London may be a big place, but like any other town, it 'as its ways. Bad things goes on, no saying they don't, but that doesn't say there is not sharp eyes around to notice the peculiar. If I know young Margaret—and I reckon I do—she wasn't taken nowhere, not without creatin' she wasn't."

Even Lou, who knew London well, could not know more than a limited number of people, but that number knew a number more, and so, like a river swollen by storms, the people inquiring for Margaret grew. By mid-day information was coming in. Most of it was irrelevant, but there was a small thread of news here and there to be looked into. One came from a disreputable lane.

"My sister 'as a friend who 'as a friend who says Ma Mud 'ad a new kiddie taken there this morning."

Lou put this piece of news to the back of her mind. The dreadful old Ma Mud was a well-known figure in the market and that she dealt in orphans was common knowl-edge. That the information had anything to do with Mar-garet was unlikely.

The late-afternoon papers carried a more important piece of information. Reporters had visited Lord and Lady Corkberry at Sedgecombe Place to learn in which or-phanage Margaret had lived. They discovered that at the moment Lady Corkberry had found out the terrible con-ditions in the orphanage, the Matron had been dismissed and never heard of since. The newsstands carried banner headlines, WHERE IS MATRON? and the newsboys screeched the question up and down the streets.

This entirely changed the picture. Before, it had been supposed Margaret had been taken out of London. Now it was likely that she was still there. The police used on the case were doubled. Lou strained ears for more gossip.

Up in Katie's room Liza tried to do what Miss Grey had told her. She had eaten her lunch, then been tucked up on Miss Grey's bed to sleep, but it was hopeless. She had never been so nervous in her life. She knew she knew the part, but would she be able to talk like a lady for three acts? Oh, why was she lying on Miss Grey's bed looking at a book she did not want to read, when the place for her was out in the streets searching for news of Margaret? Suddenly it was all too much for her. She rolled over onto her face and broke into loud, hiccuping sobs.

Only Miss Grey heard Liza crying, for Katie was in the kitchen with Mrs. Melly having a cookery lesson, and at once Liza was in Miss Grey's arms.

"Don't cry, pet. Margaret will be found, I'm sure of it."

"It's not only Margaret," Liza gasped, "it's me as Anastasia. I pretend I'll be all right, but I know I won't talk refined all night."

"Oh, yes, you will," Miss Grey promised. "You know you can do it. You've done it at rehearsals."

"Yes, but it's both things. I never talked refined with Margaret stolen. I want to go out and help look for her."

Miss Grey stroked Liza's hair.

"Try not to worry. Katie and I will come and sit in your dressing room, and after the play Sarah is going to sit with Katie while I walk home with you. Now, get up and wash your face, and then you can go down to the kitchen and see what Katie has made for our tea."

Lying on the floor tied to the mangle, it seemed to Margaret that after her bold declaration to the rats the rustlings and scufflings ceased. This made her more scared. Perhaps rats were gathering in force to bite her, and she could do nothing to protect herself. Anyway, how could

121

she fight rats? Liza had told her that London sewer rats were as big as dogs.

Then suddenly a hand was placed on hers, a small child's hand, then she could hear a dragging sound. Slowly, inch by inch, a child crawled into view. It was Simon.

"Simon!" Margaret gasped. "How glad I am to see you! Untie me quickly so I can get away."

Simon's voice was almost a whisper.

"I can't. She gave me a beating just to teach me what I'd get if she caught me talking to you."

Margaret tried not to sound impatient.

"But if I escape, you can too. I'll look after you."

"If she was to find you gone, she'd know who'd done it, and if I was to have another beating like the last, I'd die. She wouldn't care."

"Can you get to the theater tonight?"

"I don't know," Simon explained. "She beat me so cruel hard, I can't stand up."

Margaret heard a sound.

"Hush! I think she's coming up the steps."

Simon began to crawl away.

"I'm under the stairs," he whispered. "That's where she throw'd me when she'd done beating me."

Margaret could hear Matron fumbling to put the key in the lock. She looked around to see that Simon had not disturbed the dirt on the floor. Then she settled back in the exact position in which Matron had left her. Simon's visit had cheered her immensely. "Somehow," she told herself, "he's got to get to the theater. He simply must."

122

22. Hope

It was like being back in the orphanage only worse. There was a living room, Margaret discovered, which was used as a kitchen, for there was a kitchen range, a bucket of coal, and some wood chips. On a table there were some bowls with what looked like cold porridge in the bottom of each. Matron, having untied Margaret from the mangle, had pushed her into this room.

"That's my orphans' food," she said, pointing to the bowls, "but make up a nice fire so you can cook my dinner." She undid a greasy parcel and brought out a piece of steak.

"Where are your orphans?" Margaret asked.

"It's got nothing to do with you, but seeing as you'll have to see them, I'll tell you they're out working. They gets one good meal a day, and that ought to be good enough for anyone. What I say is, what won't fatten will fill."

Margaret thought of the miserable bowls of cold porridge waiting for the children, and it made her want to cry. It was all so terribly like the orphanage—a house full of hungry children while delicious food was prepared for

Matron. To disguise the fact that she had felt like crying, she stuck her chin in the air.

"If you ask me," she said, "I would think the children needed something hot when they came in."

Matron smacked Margaret's face.

"You always were a saucy child, but this theater has made you worse, so remember how you speak to me. Now get on with cooking my dinner."

Margaret waited until she heard Matron climb the stairs. Then she took off her shoes and crept out into the passage. Evidently Matron had a room upstairs, for she heard a door open and shut. Cautiously Margaret found her way under the stairs. Simon was lying on a pile of rags; he was asleep. Margaret decided to let him sleep. It would do him good, but when she had cooked Matron's dinner, she would keep back some gravy. That would nourish him. She had given Liza some cold meat for him. She wondered if she had found a chance to give it to him, then she remembered that Liza would be at the theater all day rehearsing her part. Poor Liza! She had always said she hoped she would never have to play Anastasia. Well, even now, maybe she wouldn't have to. While the fire in the stove was getting going she would see if there was a chance to escape.

There seemed to be only a front door, and that was of course locked. How about windows? There were windows in both the downstairs rooms, but they were nailed down as if for a siege. As far as she could see, if there was another window, it was upstairs, and she dared not go up there.

As if to remind her of the hopelessness of her position,

she heard Matron unlock her bedroom door. Like lightning, Margaret dashed back into the kitchen.

"Margaret!" Matron called. "Margaret Thursday!"

Margaret came out into the passage.

"Yes. What is it?"

"I forgot to tell you. I like some potatoes with my meat. I like them cooked together."

"I haven't seen a potato," Margaret shouted.

"I have to keep them from the children. There are four in a bag behind the coal bucket."

"Mean old beast!" Margaret muttered to herself. "Even grudges the children potatoes." However, it was no good fighting Matron until she had something to fight for, so she found the potatoes and a box with some cutlery in it, selected the sharpest knife, and sat down to peel the potatoes.

Peeling potatoes is a quiet job, and it gave Margaret time to think. If there was only one door and that was locked and Matron had the key, and no window which would open, somehow the front door key must be taken from Matron. What about the orphans? They had to be let in, and when they were in, were they the sort who would fight? She must make some plans. The ropes that had tied her were still lying where they had been dropped. She could roll them up and hide them; then, if Matron noticed that they were missing, she could pretend she had tidied them away. Although she had at that moment a sharp knife in her hand, it never crossed Margaret's mind to use it as a weapon; she had been well brought up and knew fighting with knives was wrong. But she did remember the broken knife she had found in the tap-room. She would hide that away in the top of her stocking. It might be a tool to force open a window if there was one.

In the house in which Margaret was brought up from the time the rector found her, Hannah, the maid, had taught her what she described as "womanly things." How to keep a house, how to sew and how to cook. Margaret was not by nature domestic, but she was fond of Hannah, so had done her best to learn. She had not learned a great deal of cooking, but enough to cook a piece of beef, and with two old ladies in the house, she was more than accustomed to laying up a tray. But in this awful house where was there a tray?

Suddenly she realized that this was a wonderful chance to look around. Leaving the meat and potatoes to simmer, she ran up the stairs. At the top were two doors: one was open. She glanced into the room, which smelled horrible. It was, she supposed, the children's room. It was very dark, for there seemed to be no windows, and as far as she could see, there was nothing in it but one bucket and piles of old torn sacks and rags. Unwillingly she turned to the other door and knocked.

Matron, she supposed, was standing behind it, for in answer to the knock, she shot out like a jack-in-the-box.

"Well, what is it?"

Margaret explained about the tray.

"Nor," she added, "can I find a tray cloth or a table napkin."

Matron evidently didn't want to admit she had none of these things.

"Just bring it here as it is," she said, "with a knife and fork. I've all I need in here."

As Margaret went downstairs she thought to herself,

126

All I need! I don't suppose she has anything. Nor should she have, the old beast!

In the kitchen, as Margaret called it to herself, though she added, "It's more like a scullery really," she carefully poured off some of the gravy into one of the porridge bowls and added a potato. The plate was too hot to carry upstairs, so she held it in the skirt of her frock. *Then she'll see the lace,* she thought. *I'd like her to see that.*

Margaret had intended to carry Matron's food into her room but she got no chance, for once more Matron shot out, this time to snatch the plate and the knife and fork from her, shouting, "Get on down, you, and scrub the hall."

Margaret went down but not to scrub the hall. She had removed most of the cold porridge from one bowl and shared it out among the other bowls. Now into the gravy she mashed the potato. She listened at the bottom of the stairs. There was no sound from above, so, with the bowl in one hand and a spoon in the other, she crept around to Simon.

He was still asleep, so very gently that she woke him up, whispering all the time, "It's all right, Simon, it's me, Margaret."

When he was awake enough to take things in, he smelled the food and he actually smiled.

"Can you feed yourself or are you too bruised?" Margaret whispered, "for I'm supposed to be scrubbing the floor."

At that moment they heard Matron unlock her bedroom door.

"Margaret Thursday?" she shouted.

"What is it?"

"Where's the fourth potato?"

"Bad," said Margaret. "I had to throw it out."

Matron apparently accepted this, for after some mumblings, she went back to her room.

There was no need to ask Simon if he could feed himself, for the food was finished.

"Oh, Margaret!" he whispered. "I could have eaten six times as much."

Margaret smiled.

"Just get out of here and you can eat as much as you like for ever and ever."

But any hope of immediate escape was crushed when Matron came downstairs. Margaret, having heard the bedroom door opening, was apparently hard at work scrubbing when Matron called, "Take this plate and wash it up. Then you'll just have time to finish the floor before I lock you up for the night. And you won't be alone. There's a boy under the stairs who has got himself knocked around a bit. I don't want him loose tonight, so you can look after him."

23. Queen Eliza

Everybody who worked in The Dolphin Theater was in a state of fuss and worry.

"It's not a thing I've ever done," Sir John told Tommy, "but I've a good mind to close the theater for the night and give the public back their money."

"You can't do that," Tommy protested. "The fog's lifted, but it's bitterly cold, so those who come tonight come because they want to see the show. I don't think Liza's as bad as all that."

Sir John had just finished his run-through with Liza.

"She's not bad at all but terribly careful, almost afraid to speak in case she drops an aitch. I can't think why we engaged her."

"I can. She read the part very well. You remarked at the time that she was a clever child. But imagine going on tonight with everyone talking and thinking of nothing but Margaret."

Sir John saw Tommy's point.

"Poor little thing! See her before she goes on and tell her I was pleased at the way she rehearsed the part, and that while she's playing, she'll get an extra pound a performance."

Bill Todd, usually a placid man, found he was, like everybody else, restless, so to calm himself, he left his box and paced the passage, where he came upon Sarah in floods of tears.

"I am ashamed to carry on so," she sobbed, when she saw Bill, "but I don't know what to be doing. I'm paid to look after Margaret, and see how badly I've done it. I see now I shouldn't have let her get in that growler, but at the time it seemed so wonderful, turning up like that, with the fog being so bad and all."

Bill, making soothing noises, guided Sarah into his box and put her into his chair.

"Now, you don't want to blame yourself. Cunning it was, the cab hanging around. Of course, it wouldn't have been difficult to learn what time you and Margaret started for the theater, seeing as you are as punctual as clocks. How would you fancy a drop of port? Or if you wait until I can get someone for the door, maybe I could fetch you some brandy. . . ."

"Oh, no, Bill, don't you go running off. It gives us all confidence you being at the stage door. Anyway, I'd fancy a drop of port."

Bill poured out the drinks and handed a glass to Sarah.

"It's a good thing you didn't fancy the brandy, for I wouldn't wonder if we didn't have the actors in early, for we certainly are in the news tonight."

Bill was right—quite soon the actors did begin to arrive. Bill, as he handed out the dressing-room keys and letters, passed on the latest information, that there was no news, but the police had the matter in hand.

"There, that's the lot," Bill said, settling down again on his box, "except for the extras, and they come later, for none is on at the beginning and mostly they are not on until the cathedral. Have a drop more port, Sarah? That drop has done you good. You looked real ill when I found you."

Tears filled Sarah's eyes.

"So would you look ill if you'd lost a child the way I've lost Margaret."

Bill was turning to comfort Sarah when there was an interruption: a group of children walked in with a woman in attendance.

"Good evening, doorkeeper," the woman said briskly.

"All present and correct?" Bill asked.

"No," said the woman, "one child is ill, but we have a replacement."

She handed Bill a piece of paper.

When they had gone, Sarah asked about the children.

"Who are they?"

"Extras used in the cathedral scene. It's what we call a block booking. The agency they are booked from agrees to send six children a night. If the six engaged turn up, then nothing happens, but if one is replaced, then the agency sends a chit what I passes on to Mr. Smith."

"Margaret would be sorry to hear one was ill," Sarah said. "She talks to the extra children, and she's real good to the little boy who is her page."

Bill glanced at the agency chit.

"Name of Simon Flower?"

"Name of Simon," Sarah agreed. "I never heard his other name."

In Margaret's dressing room Miss Grey and Katie had done what they could to comfort and cheer Liza, but it had been hard work. She was scared of the part and so

131

worried about Margaret that it hurt. However, at last she was made up and dressed and was called for her first entrance.

"You won't go," she pleaded with Miss Grey. "You will be here when I come off."

"I will," Miss Grey promised.

The moment the door had closed on Liza, Miss Grey jumped to her feet.

"Stay here, Katie, I shan't be long. I'm going to get Mrs. Melly to make us some sandwiches. I don't believe poor Mrs. Beamish has eaten a thing all day."

As always happens in the theater, once the curtain was up, the play became of supreme importance and worry was forced into the background. Except that she had to be careful with her aitches, Liza gave an adequate performance and everyone was pleased with her, so that she cheered up, and before the coronation scene, while Ivy, helped by Sarah, was fastening her into her robes, she ate several of Mrs. Melly's very tasty sandwiches.

"You'll have to be careful about the entrance, dear," Sarah told Liza. "As bad luck has it, you've a new page tonight. That Simon's off. I was talking to Mr. Todd when the children came in."

"What's the matter with Simon?" Liza asked, for she knew about him, having helped Margaret get food for him.

"I don't know, dear," said Sarah. "There's a lot of illness around. It's this treacherous weather."

Liza felt as if, with Margaret away, Simon was in her charge. "If he's ill, I hope Ma Mud's being good to him. He'll want feeding up."

Liza found the usual crowd of extras waiting on the

side of the stage. She saw that there was a new little boy in Simon's place.

"Where's Simon?" she whispered.

"I don't know nothin' about 'im," said the child. "But the girl who brought the note sayin' 'e wasn't coming seemed upset like. Said she thought that Ma Mud, what looks after them, had gone mad."

Liza had a squirrel mind. That is to say, she stored up bits of information in the back of her mind in case it might be useful. Later on, what she stored from that little whispered talk was that it was not only in The Dolphin that they were upset. Ma Mud was too. Now, what was she in a taking about?

The audience was kind to Liza, giving her such generous applause that Sir John led her forward to take a call on her own.

"Well done, dear," said Miss Grey. "I've taken Katie up to bed, and Mrs. Beamish will wait with her until I get back, so hurry up and change. You must be very tired."

It was then that Liza noticed that Miss Grey was warmly dressed for the street.

"Where are you going?" she asked.

"I'm taking you home. You remember, Mrs. Smith arranged it. You were told, but you've forgotten it, I expect."

Dimly Liza did remember talk about her getting home, but she had paid no attention. Home had seemed such a long way off.

"No, thank you," she said. "I'll go alone like I always do."

Miss Grey smiled.

"I daresay you don't want me, but I'm afraid you'll

have to put up with me. Mr. Smith's orders. They don't want to mislay the understudy as well as the principal."

Liza was sure from what she had seen of her that what Miss Grey decided should be done was done, so she said no more but sat down at the dressing table and took off her makeup.

Liza knew Miss Grey did not know London. When she said she lived near Convent Garden, it was just a neighborhood to Miss Grey. She would not know if Liza took her to the wrong street.

In some way Liza felt that Simon's absence was connected with Margaret's disappearance. She simply had to find out. She had to have a look at Ma Mud's house.

24. A Whistle in the Dark

Margaret had just finished scrubbing the hall when Matron rushed down the stairs. She seemed, thought Margaret drearily, to get more mad every moment. If I wasn't so hungry and if that room didn't smell so terrible, I would be almost glad I was going to be locked up for the night.

"Throw away that dirty water and rinse out that cleaning rag, then come with me. The children tell me there are cockroaches and rats where I'm putting you."

Emptying the water in the kitchen, Margaret tried not to shiver, but she had to speak severely to herself to stop. "You can't be so weak-spirited, Margaret Thursday, that you'd let Matron see you were frightened." The talking-to did her good, and by the time she rejoined Matron in the hall, her chin was high. This annoyed Matron, who sprang at her and tried to drag her up the stairs. Margaret was not having that. She shook Matron off and dusted her sleeves where Matron's hands had touched her.

"I am quite capable of taking myself up, but I am just as capable of throwing you down, so be careful."

Matron, muttering angrily under her breath, did not again touch Margaret but unlocked the door of the evil-smelling room, gave Margaret a savage push, then she slammed and relocked the door. Matron's push had been so violent that Margaret fell to her knees. For a moment she knelt like that, fighting back her tears.

"Is that you, Margaret Thursday? It's me, Simon." The food she had given him and probably a lot of sleep had done wonders for Simon. He sounded almost himself. "She put me in here and locked the door," Simon explained. "She said I was not to go to the theater. I couldn't get out, truly I couldn't."

"I know you couldn't. It's very dark in here. Isn't there a window? The lamplighters must have been around ages ago."

"I don't think they have lamps in this sort of lane," said Simon, "but even if there was, it wouldn't do any good. The window's boarded up."

"Why?"

"I never heard except that one of the orphans broke it."

Margaret fumbled her way across the room to the outer wall and searched it for wood. Soon her fingers found it. But finding it seemed to be no help, for it was so strongly nailed into place.

"Oh, dear, this is terribly firmly fixed."

"It's no good trying to move it," said Simon. He lowered his voice. "Don't forget she's a witch. I expect it's magicked onto the wall."

A witch! The words crept into Margaret's mind. A witch! That was what Liza had called an old woman. It was when she had told her that she thought Matron must have been a witch—not exactly meaning it, for she hoped there were no such creatures as witches. Then Liza had said, "Watch out. For they say they never die. Once they've had you in their clutches, they come back." And Liza had been scared. She had said she would cross the road to avoid meeting her. What was it Liza had called her witch? It wasn't Matron. Could there be two witches? She turned in Simon's direction.

"Who is a witch? What do you call the woman who owns this house?"

Simon was surprised.

"Ma Mud, of course. Everybody calls her that."

Ma Mud! How often she had heard Liza talk about her and the children she was supposed to look after.

"But why do you live with her?"

It was a silly question, and Margaret knew it as soon as she had asked it.

"Because I'm an orphan. Nobody didn't want me and for a few gold pieces she took me."

"But she can't have been here long. I mean, she was matron of an orphanage in the country where I was not long ago."

"I'm new, so I don't know, but the other children say she ran a big orphanage once and that gave her the idea of starting this one."

"I can't see why anyone would pay her to look after their child. One look and you can see what she's like."

Simon said sadly. "When you don't want a child, you are glad of anybody you can shift them on to."

Margaret felt her knees wobbling, for she had eaten nothing since breakfast, so she sank down beside Simon. If she had not felt so weak, she would have gotten up again, for the pile of rags smelled terrible. Then she made a move and felt something hard at the top of her

137

right stocking leg. Even as she leaned forward to see what it was, she remembered the broken knife she had taken to use as a weapon.

"If we could get the boards off this window, Simon, could we get out? How high up are we?"

"Too high to jump," said Simon. "But the board has been there since I came, so I don't properly know."

"But we could shout if the window was open." Margaret put the broken knife into his hands.

"Do you think you could get the boarding off with this? I am not much good with my hands."

Simon fingered the knife. He sounded quite excited.

"I could try but not yet. She's got to let the other children in first."

"Will they come in here?" Margaret asked.

"Not likely," said Simon. "Not with you here. She'll lock them up downstairs. I'll have to be terrible quiet. Can't be too careful, seeing as she's a witch."

Margaret felt again a flutter of terror. Suppose Matron was a witch! She could be. She behaved like one. Then pride came to her rescue.

"Of course she isn't a witch. There aren't such things as witches. She's just a wicked old woman. Now, go to sleep. I'll wake you the moment she locks her door."

Miss Grey was not easily frightened, but she wished Liza lived in a more salubrious neighborhood. It was such a crooked, smelly lane into which she led her.

"Is this where you live, dear? Now give me the key. I promised Mr. Smith I'd see you into your house."

Liza saw she could no longer fool Miss Grey.

"It's not my house. I live in the next street. It's Simon

who lives here and he was not at the theater, either, and I think in some way they're mixed up."

Miss Grey was just about to ask in what way when she was distracted the noise of splintering wood, which fell into the street from a window, and a triumphant voice that she would know anywhere said, "You've done it, Simon. You've done it."

"Margaret!" Liza shouted. "We're here, me and Miss Grey, and we don't know how to get in."

Margaret did not know, either, but Miss Grey had the answer. She put her police whistle to her mouth and blew.

25. The End

The Little Queen ran several weeks longer than was expected because so many people wanted to have a look at Margaret. Although, of course, the police pooh-poohed the idea, the story got around that Matron, or Ma Mud, as the public called her, was a witch. Unless she had vanished on a broomstick, how had she escaped from the house at the exact moment Grey blew her police whistle? But escape she had, though police all over the country were searching for her.

Margaret was living in The Dolphin. She was not allowed to go outside, even for a walk, unless a policeman came too.

"Such a fuss!" Margaret said to Katie. "She wouldn't be such a fool as to try and get me again."

There was a great deal of discussion about Margaret's future. Lord Delaware wrote from Ireland imploring her to come for a long holiday to stay with him: "It's a sad, dirty place, is London." But Margaret refused.

"I've no time for a holiday yet. I need a lot more experience as an actress. I'll come when everybody has heard of Margaret Thursday."

Sir John had decided to put on *The Tempest*, and there

was wonderful news about that. Lady Teaser had relented. Katie might play Ariel. Nobody knew what had made her change her mind, but Lou probably was right when she guessed that it was knowing Margaret that had done the trick.

"Nobody can say being on the stage and taking a big part had spoiled that child, so why should it spoil little Katie?"

As soon as the Ariel question was settled, Tommy Smith came forward with his repertory idea.

"There is an opening if you would like it, Margaret, for a slap-up tour with Sir George Pinkerton. And he has some fine parts lined up for you, including Juliet. You are, of course, under contract to The Dolphin, so you won't lose touch with us, but Sir George will teach you a lot that you need to learn."

Margaret talked the tour idea over with Katie.

"Mr. Smith's quite right. I have got a great deal to learn, like always listening to who is talking and coming in quickly on a cue. Oh, there's such a lot I don't know."

"Lots you don't know!" said Katie. "What about me? Every time I even think about playing Ariel, my knees shake. You know how frightening Papa can be when he thinks somebody is acting badly."

"He won't be angry with you, because you'll be good. There's something magic about you always, which will be just right for Ariel, but of course you'll be scared just as I will be playing Juliet and all the other parts with Sir George."

"It's not only Ariel," Katie said, "it's you. You'll never know how wonderful it has been sharing everything with you. I love Miss Grey, but it's not like having someone my own age to do things with. You're different. You've liked sharing, but it doesn't mean the same to you as it does to me."

Margaret thought that over and saw that Katie was right.

"It's different for you. You have a father and a mother and a famous name. All I have is me, so by myself I've got to make me famous and I'm going to do it. If I stop to think, wouldn't it be lovely to go on doing lessons with Katie? Wouldn't it be lovely to have a real home? I'm going backward. You see, I've a long way to go, Katie, so each step must be forward."

"Who will you live with?" Katie asked. "I suppose Sarah, but she can't teach you."

Margaret threw an arm around Katie and drew her head down so that she could whisper.

"I don't think Sarah's going to want to go on tour. I think she's going to marry Bill Todd."

Katie pulled away from Margaret, her eyes shining.

"How lovely! Bill's one of the nicest men I know. What makes you think they're going to marry?"

Margaret smiled.

"Trust me, Katie. I've watched. That's how I know."

Katie sighed.

"So off you go with nobody you know. Won't you be lonely?"

Margaret for a second felt sad. Then she tossed her chin into the air.

"Not really, as long as I'm on my way. You see, I've so far to go."

142